The [illegible]
Of P[illegible]ry

Ian D. Hall

Beaten Track
www.beatentrackpublishing.com

The Death of Poetry

First published 2018 by Beaten Track Publishing

ISBN: 978 1 78645 211 5

Cover Art: Cyrano Denn
cyranodenn.com

Cover Design: Roe Horvat

Beaten Track Publishing,
Burscough, Lancashire.
www.beatentrackpublishing.com

Dedication

For Judith, Anthony, Benjamin and Connor.

Dedicated to Ella Topp (1930-2017)

With thanks to Colin Dexter OBE
for his invaluable conversation in Waterloo.

Acknowledgements

It was always there in the background, the question. *When are you going to write a book? When are you going to stop writing poetry and do what you always said you were going to do?* A difficulty perhaps was that, first and foremost—aside from some very notable girlfriends who made me feel wonderfully weak and passionate—poetry was always the great love of my young life, sharing equal top billing with Manchester City, the comedy of Tony Hancock, the music of Marillion, Pink Floyd and Genesis. I had no way to answer the question; it is one thing someone imploring you to write a book, to get the stories out of your head; it is quite another to believe in yourself to allow it to happen.

It might never have happened at all had it not been for one of my greatest supporters, Ella Topp, my dear grandmother, falling very ill in the middle of 2017. It wouldn't have happened if my mum had asked me to not go to Edinburgh to review the Fringe just in case my nan took a turn for the worse whilst I was away. It certainly wouldn't have happened if the most pragmatic, most dependable man, my dad, had not said, "Write me a detective novel."

So here it is, old friend, evidence I guess that eventually you do what you were meant to do all along.

Without the support and love of my incredible wife Judith, the determination of readers who read every word before I sent it to the publisher, including Mark Luker, Tony Higginson, Alan Hewitt, Janie Philips, Paula Turner, Bob Stone and Max Rael, the hard-working and astonishing publisher who took a huge chance on me, Debbie McGowan and all at Beaten Track Publishing, none of this would have happened. Their encouragement means the world to me.

I owe a huge thank-you to Maltese poet and dear friend Miriam Calleja who deserves so much praise for her own work and who guided me round the island of Malta as I sat at my desk in Bootle.

With great thanks to Maria Freel for her invaluable insight on the subject of marine biology.

Without you, this book will mean nothing. Poetry has been my all for so long, so now, let me take you to Malta and witness *The Death of Poetry*.

Ian D. Hall
June 2018.

Contents

The time of such pleasant agony is now forever
in the lap of those who will never understand
and can only surmise what the author meant.

1.

The Woman's Story of Her Garden

SHE HAD STOPPED panicking. The last hour of her life had been one spent sitting on the end of her bed, a king-size in which she slept alone and had done since her lover walked out one morning and never came back. For that last hour, her mind had relived terror, wired itself to the subjugation of alarm, of dread, and sent her to the edge of insanity. Only a single thought had kept her from lying down on the bed and disappearing deep within its folds, taking a tablet or a dozen and sinking fast. At least this time she had not resorted to leaving marks on her arms nor cutting herself to ease the pain.

Her brain had raced through the last twenty years and seen the world—her world—for what it truly was. It was not one adorned with roses and long walks in the country. It was not one where she'd had the opportunity to become a mother. Her womb was so barren she could imagine tumbleweed, spider webs, dust, so much dust, accumulating there, moved only by sentiment, not the small forming feet of a much-needed baby.

Aside from her shallow but rapid breaths and her memories, her thoughts were the only things in the room. Time had eaten everything around her. It had kidnapped all she had loved and destroyed it in flames, passionate, deep flames. Time was an arsonist, and it had set fire to her life then watched with glee as it burned to the ground. Perhaps it watched her now, gripping its hands together, a sexual pleasure growing in its body, an orgasm fuelled by the desire of naked revenge, the erect nipples of retribution and the settling of a final score—the punishment she so surely and richly deserved.

All those times she'd hoped she had made up for the trouble, for all the lies she had told; all the cover-ups and denials of truth she had made before, batted away, strongly rejected and defiantly rebuffed. All lies; her life now consigned to lies.

The letter, which had laid in her hands for the exact same hour as she had sat on the bed, began to tremble, shift by fractions in her grasp. The writing slid out of view as the letter finally, silently dropped to the floor, though the words kept crashing through her mind, barging past every defence she put in its way. The people of Berlin once had their wall, patrolled by zealous guards but breached often by the brave and the foolhardy. The Irish were kept apart by road blocks and guns, by an Act of Parliament, yet could easily cross by back routes if they were resourceful.

Her past was cunning. It had lain in wait, let her get comfortable while it set down mines and bombs. It would only take one grenade tossed somewhere in the melee of metal and plastic explosive to act as a trigger, the catalyst for the biggest explosion witnessed. War was only a sideshow to the destruction of the human mind; now, hers was taken prisoner as it listened for the marching guard and the loading of rifles, the confirmation that Time had won.

Slowly, she got to her feet. The indent in the duvet rose with her, as if signalled by a church elder, the leader of her faith, to rise and devour the flesh of their saviour. The letter now forgotten, the accuser of her sins was hidden from view, absolved of being nothing more than a carrier of disease. *You cannot hate after the means of communication, wage war against ink and paper, an email, the deaf tone of a telephone.*

She smiled, ghostly, feminine, the resolve to follow through with the lie and not give in to the letter's demands now safe in her heart, her mind as cold and calculating as it had been all those years ago, before she allowed roses to grow in her garden, before the calm of bathing in the soft summer sun of a late August evening became her go-to place of serenity and dreams. It mattered not that her cottage was built on smears, on the rocks of colluded propaganda. Here, she was queen of all she surveyed, and the roses always caught her eye before each September passed, inevitably, away.

Her life, before the mess, had been erratic, full of shameful heartbeats, moments of distaste and, just the once, utter and complete bliss. It was in that instant of surrender that the second part of her life was fixed, ordained to be the mistress of a lover who did not care for her, who saw her only as a meal ticket, their larger-than-life presence filled with equal shame—not one based on poverty nor ignorance of destitution, but one created by sickness, a mind corroded by the acid of envy, of a fat-devouring virus that saw them controlled by impulse, by the need to destroy and eradicate any semblance of love.

She walked to the window and looked down upon her garden, the small section of Earth she called her own, a home she had made with care and attention. Anything she had loved in the days of bleak offerings, she had mentally taken note of and promised to herself when the beatings came, when her father's fist nearly cost her the use of one eye, when the woman who demanded she call her mother had molested her and left her damaged, unlovable and never wanting a hand to be so intimate again until she had met that one person—that one person who told her she was not the problem, not to blame for others' insanity.

Beyond her garden, she saw the new housing estate, full of families, crowded with children, with possible futures and questions, riddles waiting to be undone, to be solved and sent on their way, some with pride, some with love, others with a kick in the backside and words of anger, of momentary ill-thought hatred and damned curses. Those were the offspring of the generation that had it all—every convenience, every opportunity—and they squandered it. They allowed it to slip through their fingers like drops of water caressed by a man whose hands were too gnarled, too bony to connect properly and whose body shook in the grip of disease.

The morning had started well; a dozen roses had come into bloom. She had looked upon them with pleasure and with the firm resolve to walk the narrow path that hugged the banks of the London–Birmingham railway line which had once seen her sleep…when sleep came under bushes, trying desperately to keep warm…keeping people at bay, keeping her baby alive…

There was a baby? How have I forgotten there was a baby, a precious child? Where did that baby go?

The garden, so pristine, so perfect after years of careful nurturing, so many blooms gazed upon with pride and honour, faded, turned grey. She looked up, but there was not a cloud in the sky. The sun shone as it always did at this time of year, and all was well. No insects diseased her plants; no aphids chewed on her flowers; never a wasp dared enter her garden.

A pain suddenly forced itself to the very front of her head, and she put her hand up to feel for a bruise.

Who hit me?

She turned around, half expecting to find an intruder standing there—one of the boys from the estate perhaps, who had crept in, climbed the stairs and was, at this very moment, contemplating rape. But nobody was there. All was quiet and nothing was out of place—she couldn't even see the letter that had started all this confusion.

Did I dream it? Was it real?

She felt cold and turned back to look out into the garden again where the sun blazed away, the fat old sun, a nuclear storm in space bestowing life on Earth. Would it die in a rage, like she had expected herself to have done, long in the past, in the time before the garden? Or would it one day become fragile and as cold as she?

There was something wrong in the garden. Where the grass should have been alert, vibrant and full of colour, there was dust, baked dry, cracked and broken. The flowers, her roses, had started to wilt and become listless; spiders wove their entangled webs on the gate, on her wooden seat and on the table where she always had her afternoon tea. She watched a particularly slow, fat one crawl without care over the copy of her latest book, a romance, and leave a trail of eggs across its cover. She tried to scream, but no noise came, only strangulated air snaking its way out of her lungs, and her heart felt as if it would burst.

A warm trickle of blood ran down her forehead, and the house alarm went off, piercing, shrieking, violent. She thought she heard someone calling her name in the distance, but there was nobody home. There was only her in this once perfectly ordered world unravelling before her.

In the now overgrown garden, she watched her flowers die in slow motion. Webs covered the grass, and the ivy—a long, hard battle to keep that under control—started to tear apart the brick walls that had kept the inhabitants of the estate out of mind when she'd fancied solitude and air, to be alone with her thoughts and pretend the world would never end. The ivy, now heavy and full of insects that bit and chewed on the dead, brought down the trellis with a crash. Splintered wood rotted quickly into the tangle of webs and dust as newly hatched spiders copulated and fed on their mother, growing fat, bulbous and pregnant in the space of a minute. Still the alarm rang on, sharp and shrill. Danger. She was in danger.

Finally a scream, as loud as the alarm, more frightening because of its beast-like nature. Its wail, sharp, painful and intense, hurt her ears as if someone had boxed them like her father had done when he caught her taking money from his wallet, or looking at herself in the mirror, or when she prayed for it all to stop. But she could not discern from which direction it came. She looked out the window once more and gasped at the sight of the piles of decomposing leaves, the gathering insects conjoining, multiplying, increasing exponentially for each second she watched. A branch, overgrown, stubbly, gnarled and knotted, hit the window, and the smallest of cracks appeared. The glass held for a second before splintering into shards and allowing the cold breeze to catch directly in the back of her open mouth.

Slowly stepping backwards towards the bed, she watched the ivy creep through the broken window, probing, searching for her. Spiders crawled along its finger-like tentacles; earwigs soldiered past, dropped onto the carpet and scurried away.

The door. I must get out. The world has gone mad...or am I mad? Have I always been mad? How could I forget the baby?

For the first time since her teens, fear gripped her soul. She thought she'd left all that behind. That since (the baby) she had found peace. That when she had found the courage to let it go, to walk away from (the baby) harm, she would never feel terror, rage or despair again. She was supposed to be safe—she *needed* to be safe, even if she was forever cocooned inside this house, away from the dangers of the outside world, from the damage she could (cause) be subjected to. She was supposed to be safe.

She reached the door: *locked*. It was never locked—a hangover from the days when she could not escape her mother's wandering touch or her father's fists. She could run, and she could get away—not every time, but sometimes—and it felt good to have that ability in her life so many years after (the baby) she last saw her parents, when they had both been taken away. Still, it was a habit she maintained; she hated being locked in her bedroom.

What is that? A cat? A dog? Sharp nails rasped against the door, making the wood crack and splinter as the window had done, and she quickly turned away. She didn't want to know what lay on the other side of the door—the partition between her and escape. For the first time since she'd read the letter, she noticed it on the floor and scooped it up, this malicious piece of gossip, this interminable intruder into her peace, her solitude. This was the cause; this was the disease she had allowed into her life, and it must pay.

Spiders crawled over the carpeted floor, and she stamped down on those that dared to challenge her authority as mistress of this home. No escape, she rushed into the bathroom and, for the first time in many years, locked the door behind her. Panic rose in her throat, in the pit of her stomach, and it bubbled and burst like the pictures of Mount Etna she had obsessed over as a child. A dream of a life she had wanted—to be close to something that could destroy (her) a town, a city, and yet keep it for two thousand years along with the ghosts of its people, their space in time preserved for all to witness, to pore over like human sulphur and try to digest the enormity of being buried alive under all that volcanic ash, or burned, disintegrated molecule by atom by final scream goodbye, in the hot lava as it ran and boiled away the landscape to nothing.

In the mirror above the marble sink, she studied her reflection through a thin layer of ghostly shadow laid down by cold steam as the bedroom door creaked and, with a heartbreaking snap, gave way. The scratching now started on the final barrier between her and this…what was this? Death? Nature reclaiming all she had taken? It was an insect rebellion, and she was going to be the first victim. Wiping the condensation away with her sleeve, she stared deeply into the reflection, and screamed.

A spider, a small one, otherwise insignificant, crawled from her left nostril and ran innocently down towards her mouth where it stopped, quivering, on her top lip. She batted it away, slapping herself; she could no longer contain the terror that had built within.

She continued to scream as more spiders fell from her nostrils and the first shoots of poison ivy crawled from her ears, wrapping around her neck, benignly at first, then choking her, pulling on her larynx, making it impossible to scream out for help. Even if someone was there, a saviour in the darkness, they would surely not hear her muted, strangled gasping.

Her mind finally gave way; it snapped at the same time as the bathroom door cracked in two, large splinters of wood hitting her like arrows fired from a battlement, searing pain all down the side of her body that faced the door. In that moment, she did the only sane thing she could do; she smashed her head against the mirror repeatedly, and when the mirror shattered, she continued on the wall behind it until the silence came and peace returned. The last thing she felt as she sank into the void was a large bulbous spider's abdomen burst in her mouth, and tiny creatures began to crawl down her throat.

2.

The Detective's Tale of the Water

I TOOK THE CALL from dispatch two days after her death. I had never met her, never heard of her, and from the description of the way she died—smashing her own skull out on her bathroom wall—I could only find pity for the woman and for the person whose peace and ignorance had matched my own thirty minutes earlier. What I was about to tell them was going to change their life.

I waited on the wall by the ferry dock, a towering majesty crumbling in parts, echoes of a city that was bombarded by the fascists during World War Two because we, as an island race in the middle of the European and African coastlines, were valuable to their cause. My grandfather fought them; he fought in the skies and died on a foreign field that now seemed willing to abandon Malta again. My grandmother, then seventeen, deeply Catholic but carrying my mother in her belly, listened every night as the bombing shook Valletta—this island paradise that had once been the haven for knights and the playground for the rich. My grandparents had shared the agony of a city demoralised by successive waves of bombs and the threat of Italy and Germany descending upon her and raping her, ravaging her to the point of destruction. All of Malta had suffered; perhaps, in many ways, it still did.

Before me, the ferry filled with workers who could not stand the bus commute out of Valletta, day-trippers and sightseers armed to the teeth with the prized possessions of their new place in the sun. The bric-a-brac, the decorative and the same old ornaments found in a million different places on Earth, all inscribed in the same quirky font, just bearing a different name. The sandwich boxes, the muffled-down work clothes, and even the odd dignitary whom I would keep an eye on if there was time today, making the most of the rather splendid form of transport that took you from the high rise of Valletta to the modern and crazy high rise of Sliema—coffee shops, department stores and boutiques that cannot afford the rent in the prime space the tiny capital holds. Beyond Sliema, the stunning St. Julian's Bay, and onwards to the other ferry terminal that took you even further back in time to Gozo, or to that most natural of beauties, Comino.

Not for the first time in my life, I wished I could call upon my friend and ask him to transport me out to the tiny island for the day and rest awhile on its pure sands where everybody sat almost on top of each other but with firm smiles of enjoyment plastered to their faces. I had never seen anybody even have an argument on the island, never seen anyone get tearful except for the small children who could not understand the reasons why three ice creams in one day is a bad idea and to whom having any sort of fruit was akin to a session in the torture chamber.

My hand hovered above my coat pocket for a moment. I could make the call; I could be by the St. Julian's Bay Hotel in less than an hour. The day still stretched before me, and Tony would greet me like an old friend. A few euros in his hand and he would drop me right by the jetty. An afternoon on the beach, no cares, no worries, no disturbing the doctor with this trouble. I could phone dispatch and tell them I'd run the errand tomorrow. After all, I knew the doctor reasonably well. He'd either be spending the day lecturing or sitting in his favourite part of The Pub watching tourists come and look at the place in which his cinematic hero died and thanking his own personal deity that he had not been able to join in that sadness of the day due to having his appendix removed...

Or he'd be showing my ex-wife a good time out on his yacht, one that had barely moved a foot since the day he purchased it for far less than it was worth and which now safely bobbed up and down in the calm waters on the other side of Valletta, down in the Three Cities.

I have a job to do. I remember thinking that, the day she left me for the doctor—my friend. Still my friend. After all, we both had British heritage in our soul and blood, his perhaps less certain before today. But looking at him, every inch of his body screamed out fatalistically *I am British. I am a tea-loving lecturer. I take what isn't mine and greedily want more. I cannot abide anything I don't understand, and yet, outside of literature, my students and a bottle of expensive Chivas Regal, my only true love is this island to which I came when I ran away from everything else.*

I liked the doctor. I wished no harm on him—*good luck with my ex-wife*, I say. She was a manipulative bitch anyway, always there with the snide put-downs, with the glass always empty, never satisfied unless she was being treated like a queen. It only took a year of marriage for me to realise that the closest she would ever have come to royalty was back in the days when they employed people to wipe their arses. That always amused me; for all her airs and graces, she was nothing but a common shit-cleaner.

But I liked the doctor. I told myself that every day. We'd known each other for the best part of thirty years, both having worked in the same small hotel, he whilst escaping his own past and running from his foster parents in deepest Buckinghamshire, me... Well, my father despaired of me ever following in his footsteps, and the owner said he would work me in the kitchens until my fingers bled and my heart ached long enough to buck my ideas up and stop running with a crowd that would prohibit me from joining the police force.

The doctor and I were good for each other. A mutual bond of anger at the world developed into true friendship. Each time he sees him, my father proclaims him as the man who saved his son's future, and it is hard to disagree with such a fact. Yet I know as sure as I sit on this wall, putting off the inevitable conversation with my friend, that I saved his life as well. He taught me there was more to causing destruction in my native land; that the road I was headed on would have had me in prison or dead by now. I taught him that it was all right to have a home; running away was not always the only option. My mother and father adopted him informally as one of their own and perhaps would have loved to have him stay with us—my sister would have certainly agreed, God rest her soul—but he was proud he'd stood up to his foster parents and made his way to the tiny island in search of peace. I don't think he ever wanted to break the illusion and lose the comfort it afforded him.

I recalled fondly those days in St. Paul's Bay, the kitchen work, the endless monotony only broken by the Monday night off when we—the doctor, my sister and I—would head down the hill armed with a crate of beer and sit on the beach, a fire keeping us warm on the colder nights, the beer doing its trick the rest of the time. For two whole years we did that, and it was the best memory I had. My son's birth intruded on the outskirts, perhaps, but my own rise through the police—even seeing my friend graduate from his studies—none of that came close to the day I was most proud of the doctor.

All things end, even friendship, but we remained close. I knew there was a sadness to his life, one he made up for by sleeping with the best fuck in the islands—at least he never resorted to sleeping with his students. That was the doctor—always on the right side of discretion, the lesser of two evils. To be honest, I'd rather he took up with a twenty-two-year-old student, fresh, exciting, beautiful, than lower himself to sleeping with her; it was not borne out of jealousy, just loathing. Whenever I called round to see him, I'd invariably see her flaunting stages of undress while I communicated with my old friend. It was not an image I needed.

As for the woman who'd died, he'd take it badly while she'd probably find a way to receive the news in her silkiest matching bra and knickers, her body glistening from lying on the boat all day and consuming different cocktails. What a bore that must be, to just drink and piss in the marina, the gun going off at its allotted hour and time for another toxic intoxicant.

The woman who died, he certainly did not know her, though perhaps he'd dreamed of her and found his nightmares comforted by the insane distant memory of being abandoned by her. All this time not knowing…was it right to tell him finally, to put an image, now bloodstained, brain oozing down her life-ravaged face, her drug-addled mind scarred and pitted with years of abuse…was it right to tell him that she had been found? That his mother had been alive all these years in a home for the mentally unstable?

It would break his heart. He would have to leave the island to sort out the details of her death and no doubt have to take my ex-wife with him—she would not turn down the chance to visit London for the first time. But then she would be away, and I could go to places and not think about her being there somewhere in the background, seductively giving a blow job to some stranger who found her irresistible.

Thus, it was with a smile on my face that I realised I had to tell him, the man I called brother, who had kissed my sister, breathed life into her as he tried to save her from drowning in the waters surrounding St. Paul's Bay, who had cut his hand and told me to do the same as we became blood brothers. I would tell him because it would offer me peace for a while. Hell, I would make the gesture of driving them both to the airport and wave them off.

I held the phone in my hand. His name, my friend easily found in text if not in spirit, was below Tony and above our mutual friend William who ran our favourite restaurant, the son of the original owner who had worked us to the bone during two long years of penance and retribution forced upon us by a man who wanted no crime on his island. I would make the call to honour that conviction and hoped it would afford him the same peace.

The sun was at its highest point. If I found him on the yacht then it would be quick, less messy. I had no intention of sitting there, staring at her figure whilst he absorbed the news. If he was lecturing, I would have to go to his home before he settled in for the night…I hoped I would find him in The Pub; it would make it so much easier to get drunk with him. Two old friends, a bottle of Scotch, Nathan entertaining visitors with the tale of the lost king of British acting who passed away in the corner one day and no doubt looking for the latest football score on the corner TV high above our heads.

I dialled the number, not realising at that moment I had consigned the man to his fate. I could have walked away. I could have just left a text, a simple *how are you* and *by the way…* I could have got on the Sliema-Valletta ferry, jumped overboard halfway across, swam as far out to sea as my arms would take me and gone the same way as my sister, being kissed in the hope I would breathe. I could have done anything but call the number.

The doctor answered the phone with an unexpected smile in his voice, and I concluded she wasn't there, that he was doing what he loved best: teaching young minds the finer examples of British poetics, of how the world of Aemilia Lanyer and feminism are intertwined, of how Shakespeare's Sonnet 71 was intrinsic to self-belief and would they care to join him later as he recounted tales of Chaucer and ate dates. For just a second, I believed that what I might impart—information that had been relayed to me via human voice and a selection of notes to my phone—would be taken with a devil-may-care attitude and fuck-them-all raise of the glass, his finest collection of whisky spent in a four-day marathon punctuated by tears I would not see.

In the end, all was a lie; life was one great fib, a tale we told ourselves in order to believe we were honest and decent. My grandfather had died defending one island as he ran away from the crime of raping my grandmother; my father always knew I would turn out all right, I just needed to blow off steam; my sister died because I had egged her on to prove she could swim against the tide; my friend probably had sex with his students. He certainly couldn't keep up with my ex-wife unless he had some tenderness somewhere, and nobody had ever said a bad word against him or me. I still wanted her, that glistening body, bronzed and beautiful, seductive poison. Lanyer might have defended Eve, but I wanted to be destroyed by her and validated as a human being.

Life was a series of connected lies. Here, on the wall below the great stone houses and apartments of Valletta where knights once resided; where I looked upon the distant communication tower and imagined young holidaymakers causing not-so-serious trouble; where, somewhere between Comino and Malta, my friend Tony closed his eyes and took in the sway of his motorboat; where, behind me, in the old capital, a Maltese songbird recited her poetry for her tutor whilst he cried silently for a past he never knew...the lies of our existence, of our short, flammable life on Earth, festered and grew like a web full of spiders.

His voice remained bright for a moment. He had indeed been teaching—a session on British Beat Poetry and a discussion on why Liverpool was always going to be the Renaissance. He had been motivated, he said, to go over old works he had long neglected since other desires had got in the way. Jokingly, I asked her name, this new inspiration, and I thought he said Caroline, but the word was lost in the dense fog of the ferry and its passengers leaving the dock.

It was a word I would forget; it didn't matter anymore. I told him I had an important message to pass on, something delicate, he must be free to take it in. Would it be better to come to the house tonight? Strangely, he replied no; he was leaving the university grounds now, anyway, and had intended to see Marco, the broker of many a boat purchase in the island, but that could wait.

"The Pub," he said. "I shall meet you at The Pub—get in a pint of Guinness and a full bottle of Glenfiddich. It sounds serious enough to take the rest of the day off." With that, he put the phone down, and all was silent in the Valletta town.

I picked myself up off the wall. The ferry was now halfway across the seamless, forgiving bay, and the visitors, tourists and vagabonds began to look insignificant to the world. The hardest afternoon of my life so far was upon me. I felt as if I were going to bury a friend, cremate his virtue to the gods and whisper in the eulogy that this was indeed the death of poetry, that the time of such pleasant agony was now forever in the lap of those who would never understand and could only surmise what the author meant.

I turned away from the harbour, from the bay and the thoughts of an afternoon spent on the small golden beach of Comino, my own interest in poetry guided by the tawdry and unromantic, save for the line written in earnest by Dylan Thomas: *Rage, rage against the dying of the light.* I was about to kill a man with the power of illumination.

3.

The Doctor's Ongoing Tale

I LIED. I LIED to my friend, and more than likely he'll know if I do something stupid in the next couple of hours. I have to make sure I cover my tracks, that my story fits, until I can leave. *There's a thought.* In a way, it's fortuitous; I now *have* to leave. I can put the last year behind me, get out of the mess I'm in and return…to what? To home? England was never that for me. It's a place of foster homes, neglect, social head-screws and unwanted attention, yet back to that island I must go, to see what remains of my old life, for being here in Malta with my best friend's wife, caught in the entanglement of love, will destroy me.

He always said, when the beer flowed, or when he swirled my best Scotch around his mouth as if he were a connoisseur, a true lover of the peaty aftertaste, that it would happen one day. Yes, he's a good detective, yes, he's my best friend, but I could have poured him cheap blended whisky, the kind that makes a great Christmas gift for the alcoholic in your life, where the vapour that rises from the bottle when you unscrew the cap alone can strip the taste buds and rot your guts out at the same time. Blended whisky, the cheap and nasty kind, is not even worth brushing your teeth with.

He always said one day I would fall for a student, and I always laughed it off, dismissed it as the vocalised envy of a man who had the best woman on the island but whose jealousy caused them to part.

I lied to my friend, just as he, no doubt, lied to me as he called from the water's edge of Valletta and told me he could be at The Pub in a quarter of an hour. I told him, in keeping with the pretence, that I had just finished lecturing for the day, and it would be at least two hours by the time I got off campus, changed and caught the bus to the terminus outside of the city walls.

Sitting on the deck of my yacht for the final time as I wait for the sales negotiations to conclude, I wish I *had* been giving a lecture today. The sights and smells of the university would have infused me to give a stirring presentation of one of Lanyer's works. I might have gone easy on them all and just talked of the legacy of death as the Welsh Bard drank himself to the final breath in New York… *Do not go gently into that good night, at least, not with a stomachful of gut-rot New York whiskey in you anyway.*

The lie: always the smallest untruth, the dainty nugget that only comes to light when it is too late; the fountain of innocence departed and sadly mistaken for atonement. I lied to my friend, as he had lied to me, as his sister, cold, deep underground, buried many years, the broken heart within the smile of a girl, had lied to him when she told him she would prove him wrong; she could swim. Sixteen, beautiful, a red-haired wonder with forthcoming breasts who only showed off because she wanted me to love her, to see her as not a younger sister but a woman.

I hate selling nice things. I hate seeing them disappear from my life, especially when the price is way down on its value. To caress this fine beauty once more, to feel her squeal beneath my fingers, to be inside her and take her all the way…to jump in after the girl with red hair and breathe life into her as her stupid brother watches on, whimpering, full of regret but not helping me, never once attempting to save her.

I read her diary once, long after the event in the bay; long after I had worked my backside off in that kitchen and waited on tables and scrubbed floors; long after I finally received my degree in literature and my friend had joined the police force. I read her diary and cried.

What is this news? Why the sudden urgency? For all he knows about my life, I'm more than happy to have him come over to the house, although 'the ex' is always a sticking point. He's welcome to her. Even before I met Caroline, I knew my time with the long legs and the false sense of gratitude was over. Her demands are inadequate for the life I want, her shrillness of pleasure as fake as the interests she pretends to receive pleasure from. She is a woman born for falseness and lies; he's welcome to her, and she to him. I genuinely hope they will reconcile. Nothing will change—she will still flirt with half the men she meets and I will still want to go to bed with her—but at least I will no longer have to put up with her at home.

Caroline is different. She is the first woman to draw me in with her intelligence, wit and determination. She's English but chose to study in Malta because her father once met me and heard me talk of poetry. I'm flattered to be remembered in such a way, and it is flattery that strokes my ego more effectively than any bottle of expensive whisky or polished yacht. For the first time, I feel desire rather than need. I don't really desire the yacht, I certainly don't desire the fine collection of bottled heaven, the house or the job. But I desire Caroline and I'm willing to live in poverty and exile to have her.

Perhaps he was always right; I would fall for one of my students. He once told me he believed I'd had affairs with at least five of my students—for a good detective he's woeful on that score. Never once have I touched, kissed or even looked in that way at those in my care nor seen anything but enquiring minds, or, at least, minds that will get through my modules without breaking the hearts of poets around the world.

The closest I came was with the woman the local press call the Maltese Songbird—a poet of rare quality, of illuminating rage and sheer honest indulgence as she unveils every word like a peace offering. She became one of my finest students, a star of the island, and it's a pleasure to see her perform on stage. I do so as often as I can, taking freshers to her annual poetry event in aid of the preservation of the ideals of the island. To watch her talk with vigour and passion in both her native language and English is my idea of heaven, and for an atheist, that's pretty remarkable.

What is this news? The question dominates my thoughts. My plans are in place; within the week, 'the ex' will be my ex and either end up on the doorstep of a friendly face or turn to him, sleeping recklessly and asking for forgiveness. He will cave; he always does. I imagine him now, walking up the hill, slightly out of breath from the extra pounds he's put on since he became a detective, the need to fit into the uniform a long-gone requirement, his flannel trousers catching in the slight breeze, and his jacket—a particular favourite of his—pleading to be reconciled with its former glory: pristine, always ironed, always cool in the background. No doubt he'll be wearing his panama, an allusion to the faded style for which he once was admired. To be fair to him, he could always wear a hat well; it's a quality I admire and could only wish I possessed.

A week to box everything valuable together, hand in a quick resignation to the board in the morning, deal with the unpleasantness that is bound to come my way, both personally and professionally, and then fly away, back to the place from which I ran, back to England, back to the cold skies and the terminal decline of a country run by fools and which cannot make up its mind about how it wants to be viewed by the rest of Europe. Not that I care; I only have to live there.

Papers wave at me from the jetty, a smile on the face of the new owner, a handshake, unforgivably watery on my part, strong and fulsome on theirs. It's the type of handshake where you know the person on the other end is about to say, 'And what was your name again?' I've been on the end of such a physical statement once before. An old friend, long since cut out of my life because I realised too late he was a human cancer, came to a graduation party held in my honour. I had worked my arse off for four years to get to the point where finally I was in a good place. I had become part of the scene, and he'd treated me as if I were leprous.

I tried to keep in touch with all my friends during the time of my degree, but I found I was increasingly shoved out. Their reasoning that I had no time for them was not true...well, not entirely. My studies meant something to me. My friend's dear father, Hector, had stumped up the money for me to attend, and I was damned if I'd spend the rest of my life cleaning dishes and fawning over holidaymakers in order to make enough money to buy a six-pack of beer every week and spend a day getting drunk.

I hope he remembers I want paying for the yacht in sterling, not euros. I want this off the books, or else why am I letting this beautiful creature go for ten thousand less than it's worth?

A handshake is a beautiful thing, but delivered by some, it can lead to a finality. The moment that lad took my hand and asked who I was, I knew, deep down, that not only is he the biggest arse I've met in my life but he's insecure. He will be successful, of course, but he'll get there by being a bully, the coward's perfect disguise. He'll belittle those who've done something cool, something incredible, laugh just a little too hard, look a person in the eye and see their life is nothing but pain and misery, and wallow in it.

I read somewhere, about five years ago, that he'd hanged himself. He'd been caught molesting young boys in his care and was later found gently swinging in the shadow of the Silent City. I, for one, did not mourn him.

Secrets. Anywhere in the world at any given moment, there is a secret act being shared, being committed to memory and then put to the back of the mind until the day comes when it is useful to spread it around. The betrayer is not the one with the knife at your back as they smile to your face, but the one with the sharpened quill and the memory of a dolphin.

I don't tell the buyer the real reason I want to sell my pride and joy so cheaply; I don't recall telling anybody. I just put it down to a need to fund a book tour in America for which the advance wasn't enough, and claim, when I return, I'll purchase an even finer yacht to sail around the islands, or at least to sit and look at the Valletta skyline and ponder Shelley and Thomas, return to the days when a flourish of conversation with Marco at the bar was the ultimate wind-down for every student except Caroline.

The money changes hands, every note present and correct, and with my savings and the pay-off I will surely receive from the university, I'm leaving with at least a quarter of a million pounds in my pocket. The sale of the house I have not yet considered; it will do no harm to think that one day I may well return. Give it a few months and the scent of the island captured in a book might stir fond memories; a letter from The Songbird might rekindle my passion for the place, and I can return. Not to teach—that avenue is fully burned, my own death of poetry gone up in small scandal and a kiss shared—but perhaps to write books. Poetry is one thing, a zeal that has carried me all my life, but to settle down and write a book while overlooking the beautiful harbour of St. Julian's Bay, Sliema or Valletta? Now, that is a big adventure.

I've lingered long enough in this place; the yacht is mine no more. I have nothing of importance here save a drink with my friend as he puts on a brave, determined face to be in the same room as his ex-wife, not knowing at this moment, as I walk down the gangplank and onto the solid ground of the pebbled quay, that she will be out of my life by the morning.

I look over my shoulder at the scale of those walls, listen to the distant sound of the gun being fired as it is every day, admire the beauty of the island, the horror inflicted upon it by warmongers, evil and tyrants, so wonderfully resolute in its ability to withstand everything the Nazis had thrown at it, that the British have stealthily imposed upon it and the tests of the modern world where it is one of the first ports of call for those running away from their own stories and fears. I pity them; I always have. To be that desperate to leave the country of your birth, to leave behind family, friends, people you went to school with, people you loved, all in the vague hope you don't drown in the waters between Africa and Malta. Between the cradle and the grave lies hope, and hope can suddenly turn sour, bitter and resentful.

She didn't ask to drown, old friend, you know that. Yet I do blame you for egging her on. I always have. I forgave you because you are a brother, but I've never forgotten seeing her face, lifeless and cold, water dripping from her red hair. I remember I was the one who tried to save her, who told your parents their daughter was dead and watched your mother drink herself into a stupor every night whilst your father became a man who sought vengeance on every criminal, took responsibility, took a stand.

Are you at the bar now? Are you sitting there cradling a beer and looking wistfully at the memorial to England's finest actor, a man with whom I once spent an entire night in destruction and whisky and crawled out to see the blinking of an ocean calling me home?

I don't know what your news is, my dear old friend, but somehow I doubt it will top mine. Caught with a student, albeit over twenty-five, in an embrace. Caught by the dean and her father, my friend. My life has always been an illusion, and yet Caroline, for a brief time, made it oh, so real. I am not the scared young lad who made his way precariously into the world of the island, who ran away, changed his fate. And now fate, ironically is sending him back to report on all he has done. It won't be hard getting a job, not really. The scandal won't follow me unless Caroline decides I am worth it.

We will have a beer—we will have several. I am in the mood now. I have finally figured out that to have an adventure as a boy is not the same as continuing it in your forties. Somewhere along the way, the boy you lost will grab you by the hand and demand that you search for him again.

Damn it, my old friend, we shall crack open a bottle of the finest whisky, and we shall talk as long as you want. For in a week, I shall be a memory to you, a faded, glorious memory, perhaps unpleasant yet nonetheless filled with anecdotes and fine tales. More than likely, I shall leave you my precious collection as I leave you your ex-wife. You can have them both; they are not as expensive or tasteful as you have been led to believe.

4.

The Ex-Wife's Tale: Her Last Diary Entry

I TRIED ON MY new skirt today. It fits well and complements my figure, not that he'll notice when I wear it next at lunch with him. To be honest, I'm not sure if there will be another quiet and gentle meal again in his presence. I'm damn sure that dinner tonight, should he come back, will be the raging storm I knew one day would finally hit our relationship.

I saw him today in Valletta, just a hint of concern etched upon his face as he wandered past me on his way, I presumed, to his favourite bar. I was enjoying late shopping, some time alone in a throng of holidaymakers and sightseers, a moment of peace spent wandering idly, aimlessly and without a care. Not that I have cared for a while. I openly admit, my friend, that my net has been cast in other directions, that the spark I once felt in the near illicitness of our time together has diminished...that another man I met innocently has become my confidante and friend. He has done more for me than the puffed-up doctor and my ex-husband could have ever done.

Do not judge me. Do not satisfy yourself with keeping a guarded smile upon your face, my long-standing guardian of secrets, for you know exactly what I am like—the Devil in a short skirt and sheer black stockings. It is how I have made my way in the world since I was fifteen.

I had my back to the main street and nearly didn't see him, his swagger, confident, bullish, the high and mighty lecturer to whom the world of literature was only a second god; money was always going to be his first. On that score, I guess I could hardly blame him. He was a refugee of sorts, a boy who arrived with almost nothing in his pocket and made a success of his life here on *my* island. I was born here, raised here, schooled here and refined here, all upon this rock stuck between Italy and the coast of Africa. Yet I am the one made to feel as if I have climbed off the back of a boat and found peace, solitude, a level of comfort without having to resort to a life of being on my back with legs in the air.

I watched him in the reflection of the department store window as he sauntered by. The smile was the same, the self-satisfied grin he never knew he was wearing; he's had it ever since I first met him, and it's always there, always damning. As he passed, my phone rang, and seeing the name light up the display, I immediately understood the smile. I knew exactly that he had sold the yacht. He'd been threatening it for months, and whilst he was unaware that I knew the reason behind it, I truly didn't think he would finally go through with it and make good on his word this one time.

Why the hell would he get rid of the yacht? Unless, of course, he's going to leave for good. The house isn't up for sale, that much I am sure of. Perhaps it's just temporary. He's been caught, knows his time at the university will imminently be curtailed and needs money to tide him over. He won't be out of the profession for long. A rap across the knuckles, that's all. He's too much in demand, brings too much money into the establishment. I just want him to suffer.

Insufferable man, just like Antonio, just like Hector, all concerned with their image and their stock in the life of the island. If it's possible to fall for a man and then utterly despise him over time, I seem to have cornered the market. I seem, my paper friend, to have realised that the men I've chased since I was a teenager have all been, in the long run, utterly tremendous let-downs.

I followed him for a minute or two until I saw him go into The Pub, all the while listening to my friend telling me he'd witnessed the transaction, that money changed hands and, just to keep me aware, it was very much under the market value for a yacht of its particular class. I made my apologies, turned off my phone and stood outside The Pub for a moment. I heard him greet Antonio with their usual brotherly admiration, a hint of sarcasm in my ex-husband's voice which I was always sure was tinged with a quiver of jealousy, a measure of envy I enjoyed hearing. Even when I was in bed and he would take a call from Antonio, I would have to stifle a laugh at that tone of voice. Yes, Antonio loved him like a brother, but there was a healthy amount of dislike, even a shred of hatred, in his mind also.

The barman came out and caught me lingering on the pavement outside, bemusement and suspicion in equal measure on his face as he stood still for a second. I bade him silently to stay quiet, not to say a word, and whilst he was completely loyal to his favourite customer, there was an understanding that he would, on this occasion, keep his counsel. It was strange, my paper friend, the look he gave me, almost born of pity, that the reason for this meeting in the middle of the afternoon was not out of a need to fill the void in his life but because a secret had been divulged.

Empathy—I have never quite got my head around this feeling so many ascribe to, and yet, for the first time in months, I felt sorry for the man I had helped to take down and for my part in it, in both their lives, the detective and the lecturer, bound by circumstance, by loss and determination, closer than any brothers I have ever met. But there was always something between them, something that had happened in the past that kept them distant, something I know I instigated without even realising, and the guilt would forever eat at my soul.

No doubt they were in there right now, doubled over with laughter at my expense, congratulating each other, the past years all one big joke between a Maltese detective and a man from whose tongue poetry dripped like honey and whom women loved, yet he could not bring himself to let go and was now screwing me over. My sympathy evaporated quickly as that dark sentence whispered in my head. *It's me or him*. I'd already agreed it wasn't going to be me; whatever was coming to him, he fully deserved it.

I couldn't resist the urge to take one last look at the man before he was crucified before the crowds. That secret smile I would wear when I next saw him on the news in his disgrace, his chapter-and-verse finale; his epitaph I would happily write, so much more succinct than one of his lectures, always fawning over the details of Shelley's ode to The Mighty or Dylan's insane poem about a day in the life of a sleepy Welsh fishing village. My rules, my words. *Here lies the career of a narcissist, be warned of those you let go.*

Neither man saw me; neither looked up from their earnest conversation. They sat, side on to each other, huddled as if plotting the downfall of governments, but I could see from just a few seconds' observation, a few moments spent looking at the one eye in clear view, that he had been crying. In all the years I've known him, in all the time we've spent together, firstly as friends, then as lovers, I have never witnessed a single tear fall down his face, not at Antonio's sister's funeral, not when he graduated and certainly not at the death of his own child. A cold steely resolve has haunted this man, for all I know, for all his life.

What makes the man? I wonder. I have known uncomplicated men. I have known them to be as weak as they are charming. Since the first time I undressed willingly in front of a man, I understood their belief in their own power, but as soon as they come, as soon as they dispense their gift of testosterone, they become stupid and ineffectual. They will bark and behave like a dog if your need pleases them.

Control—it boils down to keeping them in check, and I certainly can. It's easy with a man like Antonio, a man who lives in his father's shadow, who cannot see the light of day nor his own potential, limited as it is, to become just as good a man as his dear detective father whose sternness was only briefly replaced by joy when the good doctor came into his family's life, and then by a terminal sadness, unseen for the most part but always there in the background, when his daughter drowned in the bay, her red hair as radiant as her body was lifeless. This was the measure of the man's weakness, his beloved daughter even in death outshining his son.

Again, I felt a stab of pity when I saw that legend of a man with tears streaking down his face, a muffled cry of desperation as he slung back in his chair, and for the briefest of seconds, I swear to whichever deity looks after my soul, he saw me. No movement was made by either of us. I froze, as did he, the tears still running down his face—I hope—blurring his vision and blinding him to the truth that I'd been spying on him. Would he figure out the day's events? Would he realise the yacht sale was tainted?

I broke first and ran down the narrow cobbled, high-walled street, turned left, passed the unsurprised and unmoving guards on display outside the Parliament building, onto St. Lucia's Street and down the hill to the ferry terminal. I had not run in years and, whilst still pretty trim for my age, the experience was not one I wish to repeat for the rest of my life. So caught up in the momentary betrayal, so seized by my need to see a man destroyed,

I could have run straight across the bay and been revered as an internet fraud, a magician who found a way to beat Canute and Jesus in the modern photographic age.

Catching my breath, pained from the unwanted and unwarranted exercise and shamed by my own surprise at being found spying on a lover—on two lovers—I looked up the long, rambling hill. The large and, in some cases, crumbling-down apartments that had survived the beast of war looked as decayed as my virtue, as frayed as my soul and as thoughtless to the unseen eye as my breathing. It was only then I realised—when I had, out of panic and out of pattern, headed to the wrong side of the capital—that my home was not with the doctor.

I was, effectively, homeless for the first time since I was a young teenager living from day to day, selling trinkets, baubles and postcards I would steal from outside of shops. With polite ease and a cheeky adorable smile, I took tourists' hard-earned cash, sometimes going further if they looked rich enough—didn't matter if they were good-looking. If they had the cash, I'd sell more than a trinket or fruitless snow globe.

As the ferry made its way to dock, the water rampaging forth under the weight of the hull only to be pushed away as if it were nothing, inconsequential with no meaning and certainly no memory, I realised, my faithful friend, that I had the key. I knew there was a lock and a concierge who kept tabs on all he surveyed. I would be safe there, at the doctor's apartment—our apartment away from the country setting he so loved. It was mine to have, at least for the night. He would not come back here.

Whatever was going down, whatever had made the stoic professional cry like a ten-year-old boy hiding in the shadows of his room, he would want to be surrounded by his books, those pages of poetry he often quoted and which made young students' hearts flutter with joy. He would probably immerse himself in a couple of chapters of *Moby Dick*, pretend for a while the whale consuming him bit by bit on this night was open to revenge. He could tame the wild beast of the sea and, like the ferry, discipline the water to be submissive to his will.

That was the only part of his life I could fully understand, the only part where he showed emotion. He would not want to return to the apartment, the cold and the sterile, not a single written word to be found except the odd letter from a neighbour inviting him in forlorn hope to a party, or dinner, to have a piece of his time and hear him talk about his life and the weeds that grow within it. There would be no going across that stretch of water tonight. There was safety across the bay, the only ghost that of a red-haired girl whom I befriended and allowed to drown.

***

The sun is leaving us for another day. I have spoken to my new man and told him where I am. When he gets back to the island tomorrow, when all is sorted on his end, I can start work on seeing the man I loved slowly disintegrate. How dare he treat me in such a way, cut me loose when I have done everything I can to make his life easy? I confess I long to see it happen now; I desire nothing else but to see him humiliated, brought down and shamed. Will he leave the island? Will the scandal be too much for him to bear? I don't wish to see him die, let me be clear. However, let us see that pride pricked; let him suffer for all the times he spoke with gentleness to a woman and then left her hanging.

Death comes in many forms. For one such as the doctor, it will, I have no doubt, be a release. His friends will cover up all he has done, his past unscathed. Yet if he were to be embarrassed over and over again, they would drift away, leaving him with nothing but a bottle of his treasured whisky and the memory of me.

I close the book on you tonight. I wish to enjoy the air outside, always so thrilling as it races through the watery passage that separates Europe from Africa. I will raise a glass to you, my friend. Our purpose is nearly complete, and tomorrow brings a new dawn, a recollection of what went before and time to savour it.

I am not that girl anymore, who sold beads of glass on the beach, who sold herself to tourists, who gave away trinkets for a bed. I am not the unwanted or the distasteful who had to earn a smile from a policeman just to seek protection from a beating. I am not her. I am still the one who urged a young red-haired girl to her death. I cannot escape that. But tonight, I will look far beyond the horizon and love every minute of what remains of the day.

5.

The Student's Tale: A Confession, of Sorts

I AM FULLY AWARE of my part in the doctor's downfall, but let me tell you this: I have only a few regrets, and whilst we are all starved of meaningful purpose in this ever-expanding society, whilst we become more and more a shuffling number in a sea of millions only content to party and breathe in the atmosphere of the so-called great and the good, some of us wanted more. *I* wanted more; I wanted a great deal more.

Two men with different outlooks on life, both proposing a plan of action to me…of course I was flattered. I was bowled over for a while, that these two men might desire me for very different reasons. One, a truly gifted lecturer who made people feel the passion of literature, the other, a man with the anger of truth burning inside of him to whom legitimacy meant everything. To him I was drawn, only because his integrity seemed unquestionable, yet by taking his hand and joining him on his quest, I fell for the other, unexpectedly, unashamedly and without a tinge of regret.

Regrets—what are they but chances missed, the scorned and the spurned to whom positive light detracts and makes jealousy a real entity? By and by, they come in waves when your mind is filled with less than perfect ideals. They scrabble around your brain, in between the dark knots of matter and the searing heat produced by crossed wires—these are the moments when truth haunts your dreams.

Whether you find yourself thinking of that one person you wronged or accused of doing something despicable, or who did you the worst disservice, perhaps took time out of their life to run you down, spread rumour or false anecdote about you, gripped your hand in friendship then, like an old Roman politician, seized the moment to plunge the dagger and took glee from the blood that ran down your back…

The broken friendship, the casual acquaintance lost because of a word spoken out of place, the hasty social media message that caused offence, the kneejerk reaction…

All come down to regret.

Plucked from obscurity like all the great stars—that is how I see my role in this story. In a different age, I could have been a celebrated actor, a genuine contender for awards and gossip columns. This was to be my life, but held within the confines of a university campus and in the hands of two men.

I was sitting on the steps of the old bombed-out church of St. Luke's in Liverpool when a man dressed in an ordinary plain shirt and tie, trousers and a faded blue suit jacket approached me. The hint of a smile on his face suggested a friendly demeanour but one that was filled with curiosity shrouded in politeness and interest. He held his hands open to show no malice was intended and asked if he could sit near me. The afternoon heat was in sharp contrast to the April shower the city had endured that morning, and the puddles at the bottom of the steps had already begun to evaporate.

The shoppers were out on Bold Street, as I imagined they were down in the city centre and throughout the suburbs, playing games, making the most of life and spending what they didn't have in the hope of a brighter tomorrow, whilst I sat on the steps, my hair unwashed for several weeks, my skin itchy as if filled with creatures too disgusting to contemplate, my eyes feeling as if they had sunk too far back in their sockets. I was a mess, and yet this man approached me with a semi-smile upon his face.

Telling you this now seems stupid, like it happened to another person—I look so much better now, don't I? A glow about me, a change for the better—and I see you're thinking, if not for the charges against me, you could imagine yourself sleeping with me. You would treat me like a princess before treating me like a whore.

I hope that tape is running. I hope it captures my thoughts because you, Detective, in a suit that probably cost a few hundred euros, with a nice car parked outside the station, a babe magnet, a speed demon roaming through the lanes of Malta, you sit there and dream of taking me, of fucking me. It's all over your face. You want to concentrate and get me to confess to something I didn't do, but in reality, in your heart, the only regret you have at this moment is that you have to be professional and abide by the rules. You have to treat me like a suspect.

I believed him, of course, when he said he wanted to take me off the streets, that the runaway life I had chosen was not for me. Not to sit and beg, hold out my hand or my chipped mug in the hope that someone like you would feel my anguish and pain and spare a few pence, a pound, a smile or even a comforting word. I never asked to be in the situation in which I found myself; I was put there by the damned and the irresponsible—those who believe the young are nothing but trouble. A Victorian attitude but one that still exists.

I also believed the doctor when he said he loved me. That, despite my age, he knew for the first time he had found someone with the same enquiring mind he once had. That he could get me to the point he was at. I believed him when he gave me attention, when he pushed me to expand my mind in the search for poetic form, but too soon I felt dirty. I felt the distaste of it all. He was old enough to be my father, old enough to *not* prey on a young woman. Like all men, Detective—you, my paid-for lawyer, the doctor—you all think the same thing. Take a girl off the streets and it gives you the right to own her, to dress her up like a doll and make her perform her tasks like a puppet, an extension of your own genetic code. Well, I am not a doll. I am not some dancing marionette with rouged wooden cheeks and strings attached to my hands and delicate feet. I entered into this of my own accord, and now I shall pay the price. I shall splinter as I have cut my own strings and looked into the eyes of the puppet master.

Though I pity the doctor. He's a tender man when you get him talking about poetry, when you engage with him about literature and especially whisky. There was a class towards the end of last October, a small tutorial on the effects of nationalism on poetry, and he spent the whole hour cradling a small glass of whisky whilst staring into each student's eyes, He was searching for something, a meaningful phrase that might pass their lips, the recognition of an island race invaded across time by those with empire designs on their mind, driven by their urge to rape and pillage and take what didn't belong to them. Nobody offered a tangible sentence in response, their first-year minds more concerned with not looking foolish by making a mistake, by not seeming to be out of place in a university setting.

I didn't have a clue, but something in me stirred. I saw into those enquiring eyes and fell for the mind—the man came later. I so wanted to impress him, to at least have a go, so I brought up the idea of Sappho—the epigram, 'make love not war'—and whilst I got the whole thing wrong, it endeared me to the man. He had no time for the silent type who only wrote down what they had to in order to pass the course. He wanted to see your brain working, formulating an idea and then realising that, like him, you knew nothing. That was the test, to recognise that whilst at sixteen, you think you understand the world, by the time you're twenty, you appreciate you know nothing.

My part in this deceit you have already guessed, Detective, and as you sit there making notes, watching and hoping I trip myself up and reveal to you the name of the man who first approached me on the steps of St. Luke's church, who saw past the effects of living on the streets or perhaps just wanted a puppet of his own to control, know this: I will tell all that I know, but his name is a mystery even to me. Of course he introduced himself, but, like everything else in this sordid tale of lies, slander and misrepresentation, we only acknowledge those we serve in the dark by the grip they have on us, and his grip is very tight. I will probably not survive leaving this station. Out there on the streets of Valletta is a man or a woman with a gun, and their job is to silence me. Such is his fury, his anger at what the doctor did so long ago, that all the good the man has done since he first came here, all is but an illusion obscuring the boy he was.

I have been drawn further into the spider's web. I am now one of the flies tangled up in the silk strands, and yet I do not fight like the others. I understood my fate from the moment I allowed the man to sit next to me and offer me hope. The web closed around me, and I believed I was another spider hanging on the edge of a string, but now I see I was a fly, a creature to draw in a tastier morsel. I have no shame for allowing him to place his hand upon my bare legs which had all too quickly become accustomed to the Mediterranean sunshine, to hold my face up to his and kiss me gently on the lips. I have no regrets for that, because it happened. I consented, though inside I ached, and the further I fell, the more tightly the web wrapped around me.

My benefactor—the man who clothed me, fed me, made me wash several years of grime from my body and my soul—now had me take the fight to the doctor, a man who had opened my mind to new strange thoughts. He wanted me to ensnare the doctor, use my powers of persuasion to lead him into the trap that would be his downfall. I was to get him alone, in his rooms preferably, and be caught by a member of staff and my benefactor posing as my father, with very little room for explanation or manoeuvre. An easy plan to follow, a sure thing in which one man would be so outraged he would demand the head of the other. A foolproof plan…if not for one tiny fly with a mind of her own; I had already slept with the doctor once.

Don't look at me like that. I see your face crumple. The fiercest and sturdiest male brow cannot withstand the shock of female sexuality, of a woman assured in her ability to make a man have sex with her. You all think you're in control, that you are the puppeteers of this one-act play, this performance that usually ends in defeat or subjugation. Yes, I had sex—would you like me to repeat that for the tape? I had sex with the doctor. I used him, and I enjoyed it.

A week before we were found in his rooms in the most compromising of positions, I went to his home and we had sex on the dining room table. The woman he's with was out, on the prowl herself, no doubt. He told me that, you know—said she's a horrible creature with whom he found himself, and with only as a measure of regrettable spite against a friend. Some friend. He lied all his life about who is he is and yet can command such loyalty all because of a simple act.

I know, for example, he tried to save the life of a young girl, a detective's daughter—perhaps you knew him. Perhaps she was a friend of yours once, but this girl—she died trying to swim. She was drunk, and she drowned. The report of her intoxication was hushed up, but it's still knowledge that's out there. My benefactor never told me this story, you see. I found a diary in the home of the man I was meant to destroy. On those pages was no sign of regret, no semblance of grief or apology. I knew this was the writing of a person who was absolutely and irrevocably without peace in their heart because they had spent their lives believing it not to be their fault.

I could have confronted the doctor with my discovery, but I kept it from him. He, too, was an injured party in this sordid affair, but I went to see her. I found out where she stayed most nights and confronted her with it. The truth exploded out of her like a detonated bomb. There were casualties everywhere, vitriol ejected like napalm, and in my hurry to escape the onslaught of wrath, I could only pity the doctor. I could understand why he had grasped at the straw offered him, and if I regret just one thing in all of this, if I have to apologise for a single thing, Detective, then it is only for not telling him about what I discovered in that leather-bound diary.

So, you see, Detective, my part was very simple. I lured the doctor into a trap, the final reason for which I do not know, and yet I think I have an inkling, an insight if you like. Oh, your face, Detective. I see you are interested. Well, then.

We all have a past, and we all have to either pay for it or live with it, yet nobody really knows about the doctor's past, do they? They know he came to the island as a young teenager full of anger and resentment. They know he worked silently and diligently in both the restaurant and in his studies. He tried to save a young girl's life and failed, and yet there's so much before that, isn't there? There was a life, an even angrier boy with a secret, a boy with fear of being exposed. What did he do, Detective? What did he do?

That is all I have to say. You can either lead me to a cell or take me outside and wait for the inevitable bullet to come and take me home. Perhaps it will look like an accident, perhaps even it will be you—a quick shove down the stairs that lead to the outside world, my neck broken, silenced, dead.

I wouldn't put it past you. You've gone a funny shade of red since I started talking about the woman in his life, the long since drowned girl. It's almost as if you know the story—who are these people to you, Detective? Have I been played as well and you are the final spider in my sorry tale?

Well, I didn't see that coming. I never expected two tarantulas to fight over my fly-like carcass. I never anticipated the battle for my soul. Do I regret being picked up by a smooth-talking man who offered me an opportunity to fight back at a system that had left me homeless and as dirty as the government that implemented it? Not a bit. I don't do regrets, but as I leave this confession on a tape which could be erased, when I never truly got introduced to the lawyer sitting beside me as I have freely given you this knowledge, I am suddenly afraid.

Let the tape pick this up.

I am afraid for what could happen next but comfortable with my decisions throughout the last eighteen months or so. I would not change a single day of it.

Come now, Detective, lead me on to my cell or to my destruction. This dirty angel has come to realise she is dead either way.

6.

A Dead Girl's Tale: The Reason for Swimming (Locked Away)

I WANT, MORE THAN anything at this moment, for him to be surprised. I want him to know I am willing to overcome my fears so he will look at me the way he looks at my brother: full of admiration and pride.

I cannot swim...or rather, I have not been able to, but I met someone—a young girl who looked like she needed a friend as much as I required the attention of a boy—who took time out of their life to show me the rudiments of the art and who listened to my reasons without mocking me and making me feel small.

Tomorrow, and in the pastimes of adventures to come, I will show him that the water no longer holds fear for me. I shall jump in and swim to shore quicker than they can row their boat, and I shall laugh at his surprise. I will imagine him running up the beach to hold me, but that is my second hope, for as I stand on those pebbles and feel the small grains of sand tingle and wedge themselves between my toes, I will shout to the Maltese heavens that I did it. I beat my fear.

We are surrounded by water, from the womb to our deaths here on the island, and yet some never venture into that which feeds us and saved us from invasion during my grandmother's time. The imagination talks loudly to us—*dip your toe into the water but do not venture out into the void.* It is alien; nothing good can come of it, for in the shallows lurk creatures that bite and nibble at your confidence. Gamble by going out further, fall into the dream of being able to leave the island and go elsewhere by boat, to Gozo to see something new, converse with someone different, then that alien becomes a monster.

You are conflicted. You want to be brave, to explore far beyond the Valletta skyline, go travelling just as the boy did and find life exists at the end of a gangplank, but the fear, always the fear, rises up like a shark smelling blood and sends messages to the brain that somewhere above is a person in trouble. Yes, I know they think we are sea lions or some sort of mammal in distress, but it all boils down to the same thing: we are food for beasts with teeth, the main course in the underwater restaurant.

I want him to be surprised. I have put off going across to even Comino with him. I have stayed here whilst the boys have gone over and laughed and joked with young women from all over Europe. I have felt the burning anger of jealousy when my brother tells me of the kisses our mutual friend has received from other girls. Far from the moody boy who first landed on our island, this confident and daring young man has become a magnet to those at whom he smiles.

He smiles at me. I sometimes even see him smile when he thinks I cannot see him. I appreciate the gesture—I love the feeling of embarrassment in us both—for I am almost swamped by his smile, and the waves of young lust overtake me. However, until I learn to swim, I am not going to get that kiss, let alone the pride I so long to feel.

I have been that fearful, that afraid of the water, I always ride the bus from our home into the narrow streets of Valletta rather than take the scenic route across the bay by ferry. I knew I would be safe if my mother or father were with me. Even my annoying brother held some thought of security…like a policeman asked to look after an open cell holding a crazed criminal and only having a truncheon to keep the public protected. It wouldn't be a stretch for him to push me and then say loudly, "Don't worry, I saved your life."

The water holds fascination. It is so beautiful to look at when viewed from relative safety, from a vantage point where you cannot get hurt. My mother once told me, in confidence, the same could be said of love or sex. She was drunk at the time, so I was never too sure just how much stock to put in her pearl of wisdom; that is, until recently, when I met my new friend and she told me pretty much the same, peppered with a few choice words about men in general and even more about sex.

Sex holds just as much fascination as water, although I am not ready for it at all. I look forward to the day when I can immerse myself in waves of pleasure—a different kind to that which my friend showed me when we broke into a home with a swimming pool. On a couple of such visits, we came close to being found out. Too much time splashing about, my hands grasping the rail and the warm tiles that enclosed the water like a prison—all that was missing was a sign declaring that guards have the right to inspect all bags, conversations will be taped and there will be no touching between the bars.

Swimming came easy in the end. I had a good teacher; unkempt, vulgar, unreasonable in her approach and demanding, she somehow got me past my fears, and over the course of the summer, I began to swim. I saw it as a way to finally overcome the biggest unsaid fear: the boy.

He came into our lives like a whirlwind. The sense of unease, of disquiet one felt in his presence at first was, I expect, the same as seeing a shark swimming beneath a glass-bottomed boat. You're safe; the toughened glass is there to protect you, and the boat is not under any sort of threat. Yet still you cannot help but watch as the rising soap of nerves climbs and bubbles the lining of your stomach, and you know that eventually, the temptation to break the seal will become too much. You will want to dance with the shark.

A whirlwind, a wrecking machine that landed on the island exhausted, scared and dangerous with a chip on his shoulder so wide it could span the distance between the island and Gozo. And yet, he was beautiful. A tarantula can be terrifying up close; you wouldn't want to be bitten by it or rile it to the point of absolute anger, but look at the mechanics of it. Look at its structure. Marvel at the pulse that lives under the surface. You cannot help but be hypnotised; you cannot help but admire it.

Perhaps that is it. He is not a whirlwind, of which the trail of devastation—the torn-down houses and the literary scene of a young girl clutching a dog and losing her world to the ravages of nature—is immense. Nor is he a shark, prowling the deep ocean for food, swimming and eating, surfacing and tearing apart those who seek the pleasure of putting their toes in the water. He is the spider at the heart of a web: innocuous, alluring, handsome, frightening. He will eat you, but he will do it slowly and with care. No thrashing about in the water, no path of nature driving a course across land. He is the tarantula, slow but sure, quick when pushed, carnivorous and deadly, and yet people still want to pick him up.

My brother took to him right away. They were kindred spirits lost in a fight that was not of their making. For my brother, he was perhaps the saving grace, the moment at which he turned his life around. Not overnight, not without hard work and the constant beatings by our father, determined to not let his son embarrass him by turning out to be a criminal, a cause of the island detective's failure.

He was not on the road to being a master criminal, not at such a young age, but he was a gigantic pain in the backside. To our father, he was the boy who made his life uncomfortable, hanging out with the wrong crowd, stealing, being smart with authority. One night, he was caught on the verge of breaking into a farmhouse, saved by me telling Mum what I'd overheard him talking about and her subsequently crumbling under the weight of it all. Our father caught him and had him spend the next year cleaning dishes and suffering the most horrendous time. Only then did my brother come back to us.

That time, though, was spent in the eye of the storm. He confessed to our newfound friend he had gone along to that farmhouse because he was pressured into it by a notorious family. An inside man, after all, is hard to find, and who better than the son of a celebrated detective? It soon came out, with much goading from our friend, that the farmhouse contained not only a stash of illegal guns but a consignment of heroin that had been smuggled in via the fishing village of Marsaxlokk. Drugs had found their way to Malta and my brother was supposed to have been the one to break into the farmhouse and steal all that he could find.

Almost all who were in on the deal, both the original and the one arranged by some Mafia offshoot operating out of the island, were soon caught. The owner of the farmhouse took his own life rather than face the consequences of the justice of the land. He took one of his rifles and blew his face off, the smearing of blood and bits of bone bursting like a popped balloon on the walls and dust-ridden floors.

My father took the credit for the whole operation, as was his right, yet he acknowledged privately that it was our friend who came good. Had he not coaxed my brother into spilling his torment one evening after a whole lot of plates, cutlery and fish entrails had passed before their eyes, the island might have become a plague-carrying den. I don't know a lot about drugs but I have been told about the effects. I've seen the literature been told some of the more insane and devious consequences by the friend who has taught me to swim.

My father took the boy under his wing, the moody runaway who had made his way to the island in search of peace. The secrets he kept close to his chest in that first six months, only explaining his side of the story when finally coaxed and drawn out by my father and mother. He had lived in terror and shame the previous year, driven by the suffering he believed he had caused, but my dear dad saw it was not his fault, not entirely. After all, what is a boy to do when he is subjected to such mental abuse? My dad took him under his wing, brought him into our home.

Far from resenting this approach, my brother saw it as the final piece of a jigsaw slotting into place, a jigsaw that had been ravaged and mixed up in his head until the picture no longer made sense. A once-familiar scene in which a thousand pieces had been misshaped and misaligned was now becoming clearer; he had just needed someone to be his friend.

I often wonder how people will turn out. My brother will be fine, more than OK. He just needs to be something different for a while, but I know in my heart he is a good person. Our friend...I am not so sure. The security he found in our house has made him popular, and he has an insatiable thirst for literature, but underneath is that spider at the edge of the web, waiting, patient, uncomplaining, starving and alone. He sees it all; his eyes blaze like fire and they reflect like a star, calling others to him, charismatic and charming. He will do all right for himself on the island, but he is a force of nature and will not bend to others' will, not easily, not without causing problems for those in his way. Strong but deadly.

I can almost feel the bite from the sharp fangs and the infection spreading, the bubbling of skin and the urge to scratch.

I want to kiss this spider, hold it, watch it crawl across my skin and sit perfectly still, not a twitch of a muscle from either of us, the fine hairs on the back of my hand reaching up towards its abdomen, the slight tickle, the raising of the front legs, the twitch, the eyes blazing with anger, the fear of the boy, the resolution of the spider, and down come the fangs, piercing, biting, the spider protecting itself by striking first, and yet I would still not move an inch. I would rather go numb and into shock than disturb the peace of this creature again.

I'm being silly. Ignore this young, foolish girl with dreams beyond her years. I know nothing in the end…except that the spider is real. I have seen it in his eyes when he thinks nobody is looking. He is not evil; he is just a creature like the rest of us, trying to survive in an environment that is alien to him. The spider in the wild is free. It hunts, it eats, it mates and eventually dies, perhaps eaten by its own young. However, it has been free. It has not been confined to a glass cage nor had its meat placed before it like some enclosed emperor. It does not endure the indignation of being both admired for its sensual approach and reviled for its supposed demeanour.

How like the spider he is, the majestic devil with eight legs, or, in his case, eight lives, surely having used up a few between leaving his cage in Britain to hunt and mate in the open here on the island.

I keep thinking about him, this spider in my mind. He will be the death of me, of my youth, of that I am sure, and I offer it willingly. To be his first, to be the one he remembers when he looks at others, when he sleeps with them, when he kisses them and when he leaves them. I want to be the face he sees on all those future women. I know it is a big thing to ask when I will not be staying here on the island to be surrounded by so much water for the rest of my life. I have plans to escape my own silk-drawn web and slip into the land far from stream, from river and from sea. I want to be a woman who is unafraid of sinking.

Time for me to be off. I have stuff to do before tonight. I need one last lesson from my friend. I want to be able to hold my breath underwater for a few seconds and come up with a smile on my face. I need to check with my brother that they will both be down at the beach and remember to bring a few cans of beer. After all, what is a celebration of an achievement without a drink?

There is lots to do today, but most of all, I am really looking forward to seeing the surprise, the smile on his face this evening. I am going to swim to shore for him; I am drawn to his web.

7.

The Young Knight's Tale: A One-Sided Conversation with the Beginning

I RAN AWAY. IF it was for something noble, a cause worth dying for, then on reflection, I would have done that. I would have picked up the metaphorical sword and battled every demon in my way, every man and boy that had made my life a misery, the one girl at that age I would have saved over and over again. She was a great cause, but what I did, I did because it was right, because in the end, someone who steals a young girl's work and passes it off as their own is a cheat by any name. The older student who flirts and charms their way through university on the back of lying about a tutor is equally unpleasant.

I did what I did because it was right, not to score points with the girl whose property had been stolen but because he was wrong, as was the tutor who backed him over her, and I was culpable in the deceit. Did the man deserve to die? Not at all, but he did deserve to fall.

Running away is easy. You pack a bag, you walk out of the door, and you don't look back. You don't admit to yourself the reasons why, whether they are complex or simple; you just carry on. You move on to the next place, find somewhere the memories of the final vestige of current sanity have not yet broken, snapped as loudly as a thumb and middle finger strike against each other, the human match sparking the idea and leaving that impressive digit erect and firm, giving the appropriate response to the world. *Fuck you, I am out of here.*

Running away is easier than you think. My mother managed to do it when I was a baby. One day, apparently, she was there in the house with me, content, part of a family, a dad, a grandparent still alive, all happy, all living in the same cottage, a small garden, tidy, respectable and clean. Then one day she wasn't.

I guess she was bored. The perfect life became a yawning chasm, a prison of comfort, inescapable, a sense of perfection that had not yet been earned. Her own parents had been dead for years, one murdered by the other in front of her. Her father, having owned up to an affair, probably never thought for a minute he was going to end up with a kitchen knife sticking out of his throat. Her mother, deemed by the courts to be insane, was committed and contained until the day she managed to take her own life by throwing herself from the roof of the facility to the tarmac below.

One of my foster parents once told me that when my mother was a child, she liked to remove the wings off flies she had managed to catch. She would sit at the table and, with the skill of a surgeon, almost delicately detach the wings and leave the flies without the means to escape what was coming next.

In her bedroom, she kept a glass tank, not a small one filled with childish fish, the first flush of caring for a pet that would eventually develop fin rot, turn belly up and slowly become a reminder of the need to care more and more. Something as helpless as a fish in a bowl might one day become a child, just as helpless, just as in need of protection from anything that might want to eat it.

That was not a problem for her, the protective gene. Her nurturing ability was towards the creatures in the glass tank, not an array of neon tetras, a smattering of non-aggressive platies, exotic tiger plecos or devoted swordtails. Not for her the feeding of scattered flakes and satisfaction of seeing a creature swim effortlessly towards its food, the invisible nibble because the mouth is too small to really be seen unless up close and these are not sharks, are they? These are not dangerous.

If only it had been fish, my life might have been different. Running away from the very start would not have been an option, but there is no doubt in my mind that she was crazy, batshit bonkers. Why would a young person keep tarantulas in their bedroom, even if they were enclosed in toughened glass designed to keep water, gravel and fish in tight?

Spiders. I would almost rather deal with sharks. I would rather see a dead body at the foot of the school stairs again. I would almost rather make my way across Europe again and endure the pain of running than think of her and those spiders. Batshit crazy, completely off her web. The way she dealt with the flies, losing the wings was the very least of their worries.

I stayed with foster parent after foster parent, my own father having been unable to deal with the dramatic fall of his wife, the pressure and shame of finding out that someone he loved could inject her son with heroin. How I didn't die I don't know, but he never recovered. Not long after she had started taking drugs, shared around at a party, his own father fell ill and died. I met him once; I was about twelve. He said at least she didn't pump me full of heroin until after he died. What that would have done he didn't care to speculate.

I only saw my dad once more after that. He couldn't look me in the eyes, the shame of leaving me with 'a monster' too much for him to bear. It was better if I didn't see him anymore. He was selling the cottage; the garden had become a ruin, anyway, and the once neat, ordered life had become chaos. I don't think he is alive. Like my mother, he, too, ran away.

They found her in the back of a garage, a lock-up supposed to keep your valuables, your pride and joy, all safe. They found me with a needle hanging out of my thigh, comatose, almost dead—if I was high then I don't remember too much about it. I was like the leaking battery, the unsoldered exhaust or the half-dismantled engine, bolts and nuts everywhere, mixing freely with spots of oil, dirt and dust, the unkempt but safe, out of the rain, out of the clutches of all those around her. She kept me with the spiders.

Bounced around the system, moved away from the small town where I was born and given a new name to avoid people making the connection between the baby—the child who had been syringed with heroin—and the one given a fresh start. At ten, I ended up in a town on the other side of the county, a quirk of fate I was not privy to until I met my father in the big city that divided the county. I spent a little time here and there, struggling in web after web, some wanting me to conform, holding me tight until I did as I was told, happy to clip my wings and place me in a clear glass tank, their lips moist with saliva as I became the next meal for the hungry tarantula, its body bristling, eager to have fun with the new toy at the other end of the glass playground.

My mother was an addict to almost anything—cruelty, my father, the idea of having a child around the house, class-A drugs, arachnophilia—she saw it, she wanted it, and the more she was around it, the more it aroused her. The one thing she didn't do was try out murder for herself. But then, she'd been exposed to it when her mother snapped and turned her father into some sort of overgrown kebab.

Murder was out of my mother's reach. Cruelty was about as much as she could cope with, and I'm not sure her exposing me to danger at such a young age was even cruel—not in her warped vision of reality at that time. I just think she wanted me to experience the high with her.

When they found her, she was gone, out of it completely, not even raving. There was no fight, no force in her. She had fallen so far, so quickly, all that was left of her was me, hidden by grease, boxes and the encroaching web. I was rescued, and they salvaged her, but she won't be the same again. She will be in that place forever. I hope, in her mind, it was worth it. I hope she looks out on a beautiful scene and sees the garden my father told me she loved. I hope everything is rosy, for she did me a favour by almost killing me when I was young; she taught me to be resilient.

A new girl started in our year when we were fourteen. Plain, nothing special to look at. The sad thing is, when you're a fourteen-year-old boy, what you notice about girls is their looks. Everything else, the important stuff—brains, kindness, compassion, humour—is a by-product of chasing the first kiss. You are enticed by the thought of claiming that smack on the lips, feeling the softness of the feminine allure on the brim of your tongue, tantalisingly close to the start of heavenly pursuit. That kiss… You spend ages, as a teenage boy, fantasising about it. You supplant the girl you want to kiss with the unreality, the unrealistic poster girl who catches your attention, the once-powerful pull of the dirty magazine on the polluted top shelf that houses the idealistic and the sullied, prickling in anticipation, the fantasy fuelling desire elsewhere which, at the end of the childish quest, is always going to ridden with disappointment. Name me a boy who was satisfied with the outcome.

Of course we chase the girl who looks like the centrefold. It is the look that has carried us to the point of first love, our childhood sweetheart, the coy smile, the prospect of reaching first base, and then holding that look for as long as possible, warning off the sharks in your close circle of friends, seeing the spider crawl from its hole and stalk the girl that in your mind was the same beautiful poster girl in which practice made purposeful.

This young girl was never going to be a teenage boy's dream. She was plain, but she was clever. Now, of course, all this is wrong. We are taught to be more respectful, to not see the girl in such a way, yet the girls I knew at school were just as bad. The teenage world is a lustful one. When you're an adult, you merely play the part. You act as if passion drives you, that the size of the kiss in those early days of pre-internet porn was what it always was: the tease of memory.

I was young and stupid. I fancied a lot of the girls in our class, if not our year, but I was awkward. Self-doubt for my past plagued me. I was introverted and never made it beyond a couple of first kisses, the dream of the illusion always shattered as soon as it raised its ugly head.

She bothered no one. She never bothered me—she was never on my stupid teenage radar—but in hindsight, someone in my class was always going to finally notice her. Mousy, quiet, eyes hidden away under a shower of brown hair, occasionally coming out with the heat of the sun, a knowledge of fervour which could burn into you. In another time, she would probably have been a friend of my mother's, the only difference being my mother pulled the wings off flies, whereas Lydia…she dissected words. She dismembered the confidence of the class as they tried to come to terms with the intricacies of Shakespeare's sonnets, arguing over his sexuality in terms of why he wrote the words in the first place… The dark lady… How did a man from Stratford-upon-Avon become so popular whether he took a woman for a lover or fancied putting his old friend inside the backside of another bloke…

It didn't bother me, but to Lydia, it was vitally important. Poetry was her life. Poetry was the means to make the class notice her, to understand that, whilst we have the power of athleticism, of being surrounded by hormones and dirty thoughts, she could destroy us with a fourteen-year-old stare that wouldn't have looked out of place in a badly produced film extolling the virtue of war.

When you look back at your life at school, what did you actually achieve? Did it even cross over into your life now? Did that 100-metres-winner certificate matter? Did you ever regret showing off to all and sundry, telling anyone who would listen how you were the finest short-distance runner in the school despite only going up against half the field who enjoyed a drag on a cigarette before the final race of the afternoon, and in any case you had bribed your closest rival to ease up on the day in return for setting him up with the hottest girl in school? Well, only you know the answer to that!

Other achievements, notable at the time for you all, do they really matter?

Does a grade A in French help if you're never even going to cross the Channel? Conversely, you could forgo the grade A and spend a month in Paris drinking wine, damaging international diplomacy in a single stroke by insulting the food and disrespecting the local art.

Did the headmaster's personal thoughts on your time-keeping in any way see you progress? Are you still, to this day, moaning about punching the clock, the alarm going off at six, washed, changed, out by seven and dead by eight?

My achievements were nothing. Nothing laudable. Nothing cool. The only things I would be remembered for was the death of a headmaster, sticking up for someone who could handle themselves, and causing an incident after which, for a couple of years, I went missing, having run away from a school trip to France.

Lydia's achievements would have been notable. She would have had something on the rest of us that, as we got older, we would remember with a smile. We would have toasted her in pubs—Poet Laureate, a writer of importance, or at least lecturing on the circuit. *Lydia Yates.* It has a ring to it, doesn't it? *Dr. Lydia Yates.*

After all these years, her name embarrasses me still. She had the world beckoning, but what does it matter when you take your own life? When the love you have for something is taken away from you? When a cowardly scoundrel tries to pass your work off as his own? For that, I could never forgive the little shit, nor the headmaster who lied to make the school seem a success. That the well-groomed son of the local magistrate would make a finer example of how the school had produced a wordsmith of such repute, one so young and with overwhelming talent, raw, emotional, humble but discerning, a poet for the disease of the age, the 1980s, a period of time when life was cheap, a taste of the heroin filling the veins of the young under the banner of consumerism and the prospect of nuclear war. What was there really to live for? Do you blame us for believing sex was the answer to which the question was a loaded gun?

If confession is what I have to do to solve this mess that I am, then take note. My past, my present and the damned future are all going to suffer. Sit down, I shall open a window, pour you a whisky, and you can sip gently as my life unfolds for you.

The Death of Poetry. That was to be the title of her book—Lydia's book. I published my own in her honour, I took it upon myself to continue her work and restore her name as the woman of words. Well, in my mind she was, anyway.

Sit down, my friend, there is so much you never knew about my life before we met; so much to tell, and I am ready to confess. That is, after all, the reason you drove out to see me tonight. It wasn't to make sure I got the plane in the morning. I intend to bury her, you know. Both of them. Lydia for the sake of my sanity and my natural mother for the sake of the past.

Do you remember the day you first met that small boy? Such a tired and exhausted child who had made his way through a couple of countries, who got on a train from Paris with no idea where he was going, who confronted a man for his lies, the cover-up of a suicide and the theft of a girl's life, who saw him tumble down the stairs…

Do you really want to play this game?

8.

The Detective's Tale (Continued): The Body in the Apartment

SHE WAS GONE. Well, technically, as I sat on the harbour wall opposite the new expensive apartments that had gone up along the coastline from Sliema to St. Julian's Bay, with the afternoon sun baking my arms and the small hairs on the back of my neck smouldering, none of it helping my current mood, she hadn't gone. Not yet. Her crumpled, as if unironed, body was still on the bed, neck slit open and a mix of dismay, terror and shock etched upon her face.

I waited on the wall on the other side of the road and ruminated. Only the day before, I was sitting on the other side of the bay, wondering on the best way to tell my friend his mother was dead. Now, a little after four the following day, I was wondering how I was going to tell him that *she* was dead—my ex-wife, his now ex-partner.

This was going to be big news on the island. So few cases of murder over the decades, rare enough, but this? This was horrific. A senseless frenzy and yet done with style, timing and perhaps glorification. This was a message to my friend and to me, and despite it all, despite what she had done to me during our marriage, I felt regret, pain, the overwhelming urge to rage, to stand on the quay wall and howl at the injustice.

This was not my case. I had not been called out by dispatch, but I'd heard over the radio the address to which my fellow detective had been called. I suspected they believed that in having taken the day off to help the man of letters in his hour of need, I would be not contactable for the duration. In truth, I had done my best to sleep off a hangover, self-inflicted in the line of duty the previous evening. It was a struggle to shake the desire to get on a ferry across the harbour and stroll with earnest intent up the hill and set the Devil aside for the rest of the day. I muttered something distasteful in English as a young mother and her child walked by, the accusing stare and sense of a berating causing me to immediately apologise and walk over to the ice cream bar to buy the child a treat, much to the mother's satisfaction. Being a couple of euros out of pocket was worth not having to answer unnecessary questions should she complain.

I imagined the scene unfolding inside the apartment; nothing left to chance. This was, after all, the former wife of an officer of the law, and even when a man and wife were separated, in this deeply Catholic country, the police took care of its own.

I looked up at this scar on the skyline. Once upon a time, you could see across the shops lining the parade, the long road skirting the edge of this part of Malta, the busy Triq Ix-Xatt, the old established names of the past somehow bleeding into the culture imported on the back of Britain, of Europe, of the need to have ever-increasing numbers of tourists and their ample wallets descend upon the island just to keep people in work. I never got that ideal, that sense of grand economic design. There were always people in work before Europe, before big money capitalism came to the island and we became an offshore account for those in Brussels, London and Rome. Once a colony, always a colony, I surmised.

It was not that far around the bend to St. Julian's Bay—a short bus ride away, or a long leisurely walk during which to clear the fog that was enveloping me, threatening to make cobwebs, pushing clear details out of view and replacing them with false fly leads.

The call had come through at midday; I had been at home all morning. I knew where my friend had been all night because I had a young constable keep an eye on his house. The light had been on, and, I quote, 'loud Jazz was playing'—so loud a neighbour a few hundred yards down the road and away from the cliff had complained, quite rightly. There was no way off the cliff face, nowhere for my friend to go but inside, wallowing in the devastating news I had delivered to him earlier. But still, he could have killed her. He knew people who would do the job for him…who would murder for him.

Impossible. My friend may be many things—an absolute scoundrel, a man of few scruples when it comes to stealing friends' ex-wives—but a murderer? Not a chance. It was easier to believe I would have killed her. I had motive, for sure. Means? Perhaps not. I was too drunk. Opportunity? I didn't even know she was in Sliema, but what would be the point? Life was actually more interesting, if infuriating, with her in it.

Out of the corner of my eye, I saw the ambulance arrive and park outside the building. The bus driver, who hadn't seen the vehicle coming up behind him, cursed as it cut inside causing the squeal of touched brakes and the annoyance of the standing passengers thrust sharply down the aisle. I smiled at their aggravation. I hoped they'd have the balls to take the driver to task. I knew it was petty—a thought of meanness in a world full of angry people—but for a tiny moment, it made me forget exactly why the ambulance was there.

Why was I not more distraught? My thoughts were almost consumed by how my friend would take the news, how it would affect his mind after the way his mother died. Both moments had to be linked; any detective worth his salt saw the jigsaw not as a mess to solve but knew that the framed shot cut in a thousand different ways was just the start of the investigation. Sometimes what was *not* on the box was more intriguing than what the puzzler intended to be seen.

Connected, then, but why? Christ, a whole multitude of reasons came to mind. My friend was well-liked. Could it have been professional jealousy—enough to see two women die, both horrific in their own way? Not impossible but unlikely. The scene that had greeted me in that apartment was not one of malice over a promotion issue or whose department would face cuts and have their budget decreased. This was not Oxford; there was no Endeavour Morse to ponder on the mystery. No, my favourite detective would not even dare to think this was some sort of university feud spilling over into the island's luxury apartments.

Connected. It was there, and it was nothing to do with our shared past, yet there was a piece of our history lying naked on the white cotton sheets, splattered blood staining psychoanalyst patterns—a dream for any shrink to wrap their brains around in perverse enjoyment. It had never left my mind that my friend, my doctor of words, once split the professional title 'therapist' and showed me exactly what they did to a person's mind. Though his therapy came in the form of sex, vintage malt whisky and the pursuit of women, it was hard to disagree with him.

Twice I had been ordered to seek assistance from a therapist supplied by the force: once due to the dead woman in my friend's apartment; the other when the memories of my sister started to resurface and I was finding it difficult to reconcile my own past, my actions when I was younger.

Would she still haunt my dreams, my ever disconnected thoughts, screaming at me during the night, if she didn't get her own way? Would she inhabit my nightmares with the snarl on her face that was the uninvited guest to our marriage, the hairline fracture in the corner of the memory holding up my own psyche, the column shaking, the floor ready to cave in?

She was dead now. I was free to walk around Valletta knowing I would not bump into her, that the sarcasm, the potential for her to suddenly verbally assault me was no longer there. But it wasn't such a leap in the old detective thinking to imagine taking a drive down to Bugibba and seeing her walking along, looking for shade while complaining that such an action was beneath her. I would watch the football at Paul's Sea Breeze hoping that, by the time the match was over, she would be asleep.

I knew at that moment I would never go to Rome again where we once spent a week in hell. All I had asked for was to watch Roma play. The shit hit the fan, as did her fists, and the ferocity of her argument by the Spanish Steps left me a near-broken man.

My father—tough, disciplined and at times full of indescribable rage—was always at a loss when it came to her behaviour, her outbursts, her dropping of social bombs at the most delicate of moments. When the great man of the island retired, she stood up and slow-clapped whilst everybody else at the specially invited party remained seated, watching this inexcusable interruption in the proceedings, and I sank deep into my chair in shame.

Dead now—what would it matter? I could go for coffee in her favourite café. I could have Sunday lunch down at Marsaxlokk without thinking twice and being on my guard. Fair dos to my friend, the Sundays he was with her, he would text me and tell me where they were going. Whether it was to save a scene or to spare my feelings, I was grateful to him for that.

A thought...why the gratitude? He hadn't stolen her from me; if anything, I would have happily given her away to him, a mediaeval exchange of goods on an island built upon the traditions of the Knights Templar. But it was still there. The celebrated poet living the high life, money, a status many—even in his native England—could not have dared to hope for, a succession of women on his arm, an award or two... Was I jealous? Did I actually have a motive beyond the hatred of a woman who had taken me down so many pegs, demoralised me to such an extent I doubted my own existence and became sceptical and distrustful of others? Was *I* above suspicion?

A crowd had built up outside the apartment block. Social media photographs were taken and uploaded, including a few that were not appropriate—the grin and the peace sign as the ambulance men exited carrying my ex-wife's now bloodied corpse in their delicate but hurried manner.

I hated this modern ghoulishness, the zombification of the masses as they bent their heads in reverence and shuffled along, not even noticing what was around them unless alerted by the ping of their electronic device. I hated it all, but, like many of my generation, I had been forced to take part in the experiment of mass control. Thankfully, my alibi, my cast-iron excuse, was that it always helped to have eyes and ears where a detective may be blind and deaf. By doing so, they avoided being caught unawares; it was another potential tool in the fight against crime, and if the millennials were correct, avoiding the undead was always a bonus to have in reserve.

My phone—of course! I could check my movements after leaving his house last night, put my mind at rest that I went home and had nothing to do with the grisly scene now being photographed and fingerprinted, every possible bit of DNA collected in the pursuit of unshakable evidence. It wasn't that I was truly concerned, I was a good man, weak in some respects, stupid in others, but on the whole my life was untainted by the type of anger and resentment needed to carry out such a frenzied attack. Yes, I disliked her. Did I want her out of my life that much?

I reached into my pocket, took my phone out and tapped the relevant buttons. Before I could do anything constructive to put my nerves and sometimes broken heart at ease, the springboard of messages from the general public—those hash-tagging, smiley, sarcastic-winking, red-faced furious ghouls on the other side of the road who couldn't wait for the official statement—had spread like a wildfire sweeping the island, a spew of volcanic magma destroying all that it touched. Some even went as far as to describe, without accuracy, what had happened inside that room. The truth was cinder in the hands of such uncertainty.

I scrolled through the news item. It was regimented and factual, but it didn't stop the smart arses piling in, making assumptions, commenting with their own peculiar brand of sick humour and evoking suggestions that they should become a comedy scriptwriter or comments from the oh-my-god-you're-so-funny brigade, ass-kissing buggers. It didn't just annoy me; it was in such poor taste. All the good work done to capture whomever committed this act of murder, hampered by the general public's lack of self-control and shocking display of cheering on the wrong side.

One line after another flashed before my eyes—the well-intentioned, the Rest in Peace, the off-colour joke, the additional comments from their friends overseas, the shock-horror faces of pain, red anger social media tags, yellow *slap my face until I have to put my hands up to cover the abused disbelief*, the odd thumbs up… I never got that one. Why would you signal a liking for something so hideous?

I wanted to cross the road and take every damn phone off them. Let her memory not be stained by the amusement of youth and the disgrace of those who never gave the island a second thought except perhaps as a holiday destination passed over when they realised their favourite bands didn't come here.

Before my eyes, the sentiment of false grief took over. I understood completely why many of my generation were losing touch with the young. They seemed feckless, so outraged by everything but their own ability to see beyond their own bubble. They had no idea of history, of just how close this island came to being under a fascist boot. It was one of the few things the doctor and I argued about; he was all for self-expression, insisted upon it, revelled in the ability to stir up trouble whilst holding back on complete revolution. I just wanted them to grow up.

I saw Detective Constable Aakster make her way through the heavy and, in some cases, crying crowd of mostly teenagers. I scolded myself for thinking that if they knew the dead woman as I had done, they would not be grieving; they would be fully justified in using that 'like' button on social media.

Aakster had come to the island from Holland in search of adventure, a bit of fun on the back of international exchange. She was educated, tall, took a joke well and had great taste in music—such a shame she was heading home at the end of the year. As she crossed the road, I realised I would rather have her continue working here than lose her to mainland Europe, but the island held her back. She was damn good at what she did and, more importantly, she was loyal to me.

She was carrying, tightly against her body, something that looked like a book—one without a cover. Bible-black and oddly stamped, it was a diary. As she reached me, she held it out and explained that she had noticed it hidden in the relatively few books on display in the sparse apartment. She opened the diary to the previous day's remarks—a dead woman's observations—and let me read.

It changed nothing, but it certainly filled me with the urge to vomit.

9.

The Young Knight's Tale 2: A One-Sided Conversation with the Beginning

HE WAS DEAD. Neck broken, twisted at an ungainly angle, almost back to front. It was a shame that in death he could not emulate his ability in life to appear two-faced. School was never the same after that; why would it be? In their eyes, if not in confirmation, I had killed, pushed down the stairs, the headmaster.

Do I regret him dying? Not at all. He was the catalyst of a young poet's suicide. He chose to take the wrong side in a poetic affair and paid for it with his own life. He also, many times over, abused his position; he was very hands-on in the way he dealt with the school's internal policy. Stepping out of line and getting suspended was perhaps the best you could hope for.

I first crossed his path in the third year when my foster parents could not afford a new pair of shoes for school. Strict uniform guidelines were to be observed, and yet, with about four weeks to go until the end of term, my foster parents and I could not see the point in paying out for a new pair when other bills were more pressing.

My foster father had been out of work since the New Year, laid off after ten years with the same company. Rationalising, streamlining the workforce, redundancies, ultimately replaced by cheaper workforce and machines—I think they called it progress. My foster father called it the cause and effect of allowing capitalism to run unchecked, unregulated and uncaring about the souls it destroyed. The more I look back at that time, the more I realise how naïve I was. My concern was with what I believed to be the bigger fight: the bomb, an atomic nightmare just under our feet in the countryside, ground-down dust, my future, in one blinding flash, taken away.

School uniforms—why would I want to conform to that sense of humiliation anyway? The stifling tie, starched collars, unforgiving trousers which showed just how immature you could be when you smiled at a nice girl across the classroom and she responded with a small, perhaps unconscious lick of the lips? Young lust, I think Pink Floyd called it; I called it the art of not suffering a position of embarrassment. I think Floyd said it a lot better, the difference being they got paid for it.

I hate uniforms. They remind me of control, of being placed in a set from which you cannot escape. Some take comfort from being seen in the same clothes as everybody else, the same style, the rigidness of command, a structure. Thankfully, I became a lecturer, a doctor of what I love; heaven forbid I become a teacher. I would have had those kids rioting within a month.

I think it comes from being placed into order: no room for self-expression. I have no issue with a male student, should he wish, coming to my lectures in a skirt—no more than I would care about a young woman wearing clothes more suited to the countries of the Arabian culture. If you are not hurting anyone, then why fight a battle that just doesn't concern you.

Self-expression. That is the point of it all, really: be yourself; write down the words that guide you and you alone. Don't expect followers; if they like your work, your art, your poetry, the way you play violin at three in the morning after a week of fighting insomnia just to hear a tune become reality, then nobody has the right to place in front of you restrictions so petty, so inane that all they are doing is effectively making you inferior to their belief.

Uniforms are against natural law. They stifle the creative gene, instil perverted pride and the strange beliefs of a twisted religion. Look at the British in the Victorian era, so stiff-upper-lipped, so straight-laced with their higher moral code, yet they went to war and implanted themselves as the ruling class, believing they were mentally and physically more advanced than their Indian hosts. Polish that brass buckle, Watson. Don't you know being caught with an almost invisible speck of dirt on that cap is a sign of ill-discipline? Please! Such are the ways of the fascist; it starts there, in the way you have to dress in order to stay in the pack.

Freedom is choice. Wear what you want, write what you want, see the world on a shoestring if you so desire. Just get up one day and decide that you hate the town you live in, the people, their gut-wrenching way of putting everybody else down just to elevate themselves to a higher position.

He was dead before he even hit the floor at the bottom of the steps. I heard a large crack as he fell, his head contorting at a weird angle—he was dead even before he smashed his head against the floor. I didn't push him. People thought I did, but there were none of my prints on his shirt or jacket. I was innocent, and thankfully, I had one person, a teacher, Polish by birth but who taught us French, who stuck her own neck on the line and told them she saw the whole thing. Now her, I didn't believe. She couldn't have seen what happened as the door was closed at the time. I know because I had closed it just a couple of minutes before.

I got away with wearing black trainers for a couple of days. My foster father promised he would get a new pair before the start of what would be my final year, so nothing seriously rebellious in my actions; it was done out of necessity. However, as those few days passed over, I noticed little things, moments of glorious rebellion, flowering anarchy, girls' skirts about an inch too high or rolled up like a miniskirt when they were out of sight of a prowling teacher, classroom CCTV and school jungle vibe. The girls wearing thick black tights hiding every school boy's fantasy of the black lacy knickers; black socks on the boys but, above the ankle, a figure or saying from the latest cartoon star; band T-shirts under shirts, a blazer with a pin badge of their hero... All unseen, all provoking the system from within. It was glorious; it was divine. What did it matter what I wore on my feet? These days, I would not be seen dead in trainers; I enjoy the comfort of the well-made artisan shoe, polished and looked after. I also wear blue, red, and have been known to pull off green leather shoes—anything but black. I am not Henry Ford, and I don't do conformity.

If I'd had come out of the French class with all the others, blended in regretfully as we filed haphazardly down the corridor and to the next lesson, if I had perhaps slipped my arm around any girl's waist and give her an embarrassing squeeze, then I would not have been caught and the chain of events between that day and now would perhaps have not been set in motion. But then, we still have to talk about the death of a girl and her poetry, of a thief and stolen work. Perhaps, whichever way that day had ended, I would still be here talking to you in the once-privacy of my home, two policemen outside making sure...what? That I don't abscond? That I don't go into hiding? Or are they here for my protection? Is there a killer about? Is there a person out there, somewhere in a darkened room, putting the final pieces together? They undoubtedly killed my mother, they have killed a woman I once liked enough to take from you, and now they are after me.

I had closed the door behind me, gentle, not to cause a noise, fifteen minutes late, kept back for what does not matter now, but late with note in hand, of course, and a smile on my lips. I had nothing but my wits and charm; everything else about me was based upon an insane woman's deranged sense of purpose and the drugs floating around her body. I closed the door quietly and walked straight into an argument.

His bark was just as lethal as his bite. Cruel lips, pencil moustache, trimmed eyebrows and dark satanic eyes of the kind Christopher Lee would have enjoyed showing off on camera for his millions of fans. The Devil in the detail, for in my mind, even now, he was a devil, all sulphur and burnt tobacco smoke. I am not a religious man. Since living in Malta, I've only been inside a church to set the scene for a night of poetry. How unsettling to be inside that foreboding building and deliver a line of Shakespeare, Dryden or Shelley as the sense of history, the moments of sanctuary sought, where couples pleaded for their own personal demon to watch over them as they married, procreated and brought more foot soldiers into the eternal battle between humanity and nature, where ideologies collided and were reconciled. Speaking the word of God was nothing more to me than reciting conformity. As the rafters shook and age-old dust fell like grey snow around us, I was able to tell the tale of Faustus, regicide, infanticide, genocide and all with a poetic ear.

*Look on my works, ye mighty, and despair...*for I do despair, my friend. I despair that the world is at its most serious, that we place upon our children the value of money more than the chase of love. I know I sound like a hypocrite to you. You have seen me collect both women and money and use them in equal measure, but I ask you this: do I truly desire one over the other? If I have only one thing left to attain as I await the inevitable shotgun blast and the thump in my heart, it would not be to put the record straight about the girl who died and the boy who lied. No cash in pocket for when I slipped away from the school group and made my way out of Paris, when I starved daily on the south coast of France whilst waiting to get on a boat in Marseille. None of those things mattered; all that was on my mind was survival.

He went full-scale nuclear on me. There was no build-up, no escalation, no warning of war, no peak-cap-wearing general giving a rousing speech on how the nation was in danger and a three-minute warning, no time to rush down underground and drop and cover. This was full invasion. This was the pounding at the beach head at Iwo Jima but with tactical weapons, full-on rage and fury in the face of a man whom the world would be better off without. It was the trainers at first, then came the question of why I was late getting to class, and then, when I answered back, albeit with some venom of my own, it escalated into the suicide of a young girl and her stolen poetry.

How nobody heard this verbal assault, I don't know, I imagined the young French teacher with hands tightly wrapped around her headphones, the joy of her own beautiful language slaughtered by a generation of English schoolchildren to whom learning French at O' Level was just an excuse to dream of going away to Paris for a week. I like to think, even now, that she was dreaming, wishing her next class would show some spirit, backbone and love of the French tongue.

He grabbed me and pushed me against the wall, his eyes burning deep into me, and I knew I had crossed a line. Blow the trainers; I had all but accused him of wanting the girl dead. A lonely young woman waiting to be seen as cool and inspiring but ultimately found hanging from a rafter in a local farmer's barn, nothing more than a benefit to the grief he was perpetuating, the mythical status of the wretched and how a young boy in her class was able to rise above the sadness and create such stunning poetry. It worked all round; she was nothing to the school, nothing to the parents who abused her and knew nothing of her life. But she was a shining example of how a school can pull together, and her poetry, now in the hands of the undeserving lie, is, ironically, revolutionary.

I was not tall—barely five foot six, the final growth spurt that sent me over six feet happening when I had been in Malta for a while—but I was stocky, a bit round, perhaps, but still not easy to shift. Still, he managed it with ease. He pinned me against the wall and pushed for all his worth with one large, authoritative hand, the other raised in a fist. I felt, in that moment, I was to be struck down by a thunderbolt, the blitzkrieg and the atom bomb in one swift blow.

I turned my face away and prepared for the worst, my hands down by my sides in an act of submission. Still nobody came.

It took a moment to register that his grip had relaxed. My eyes remained firmly closed, stapled shut with grim steel. I didn't open them until I heard the first scream, until I felt the reassuring hand of the French teacher on my shoulder, and her beautiful intoxicating accent, smoothed by her few years teaching the ignorant and the sex-mad teenager, told me I needed to come into the classroom with her and wait for the police and my foster father to arrive.

My head was in a whirl. I didn't know what had happened, too young to explain, but eventually the authorities believed me when I said I had done nothing to cause the terrible scene, backed up by the kindness of a teacher I could have happily kissed there and then. Surely it would come to pass that I had done something, I had caused his death, given him the hall pass of a lifetime and caused him to have a fatal stroke.

My teacher told the police how she heard the shouting and had come out of the classroom in time to see the headmaster push me against the wall, that she had heard his voice raise hell about the trainers and nothing more. Then, with his hand curled into a fist, he stopped and fell backwards, like a toppling giant, like Ozymandias, his work reduced to rubble and blood, brains and goo on the stairs.

Of the escalation in the war of attrition between us, she made no comment, no allusion, so in keeping with order, I did the same. I became a pariah at school, some perhaps saw me as a folk hero, the man who caused the death of the Devil, but if they did, they kept it to themselves. Nobody said a word. Too embarrassed to be seen with me, nobody ventured to my door during the summer holidays. I went back the first week of September to the cold shoulder and the threat of depression. By my birthday in November, I was so low I could not function properly.

It was with a strength I never realised I possessed and the fortune of my foster father managing to secure a good job that, in the March, I was able to go to Paris with the school. The chance of a lifetime, drinking in the afterglow of a European language—for the girls, the moment to shine and make the boys jealous; for the lads, perhaps with more than a slice of malice, to take the piss out of any French boy and ask if their father was German. Little minds, big pleasures.

I never told my foster father what was going through my mind. He wasn't a bad man; he didn't abuse the relationship we had. He was far too honest when drunk, and the detail he went into about my mother's own demise was arguably harrowing, but he didn't need to know that I was going to run away, that Paris was just another stop on the line. I had endured the punishment of the school, of people that I had called friends, of girls I had fancied and boys I wished to be like. I was an outcast, slowly becoming invisible and wasting away.

My only friend during that time was the French teacher, and if not for her I might not have made it beyond the first leg of the journey. She gave me time, both in the classroom and away from the hunt for me. I loved her for that; she kept my secret as I kept hers. I wrote to her once, just the once, three days after I arrived on the island. I just wrote 'thank you' and signed it. No other words, no clues—I even managed to persuade a holidaymaker to post it when they got back home, choosing someone who looked like they weren't heading back to England just in case they recognised me.

10.

The Exchange of Information: The Tale of the Officer on Secondment

I LOVE BEING UNDERCOVER. It suits me being invisible, to be in plain sight and just treated as scenery, that person you see out of the corner of your eye but dismiss as another shopper, the casual girlfriend on the arm of a loved one, the holiday sun seeker or even the damaged beggar on the street which passers-by sniff at or ease their conscience by dropping the odd euro in the dirty cap I keep for such occasions.

I like these roles, these dramatic parts in which the actor in me gets to be someone else. I really should have been an actor; however, my father, perhaps rightly but not with conviction, suggested that after four years of living and studying in England, it was time to get a job with responsibility and promotion prospects, and settle down in one place—near home, near him and my mother.

I am a spy. They wanted to spy on me, keep me close, introduce me to the right people, get me a job in the community—something that would make use of the degree I earned in England but would also have me looked upon as coming home to impart knowledge to the next generation of teenagers in Amsterdam. A teacher is what they had in mind, and I could not have been more horrified. I didn't like being around children even when I was one myself. All those tantrums, all those moments of dealing with the sticky and the thrown-down stamped foot. I admired the teachers who took us on during the week, no doubt threw themselves into the self-harm of alcohol on a Saturday night and hopefully wiped us from memory with a weekend of orgies and sex with strangers. Or is that just me being cynically optimistic as I approach the hill of thirty?

I went home after university. I said goodbye to my friends and promised to keep in touch, knowing at the back of my mind that for all the signed promises and drunken kisses of remembrance, I would be too engrossed in a job to see them again for a while, and anyway, they would have the same issues, family, career, children, pets, what to do on a Saturday, how not to care by Sunday morning. The biggest regret of higher learning is that you realise how lonely your life is afterwards.

I went home. I dossed around for a week or two as I weighed up my options and decided on a whim the police was the only option that would fulfil me. If I could not work in theatre, as I had wanted, then being in uniform, being part of something greater than I could manage on my own was the way to go.

Being part of something, but not averse to picking a side, of choosing between a path that was right and decent—to the letter of the law and sitting it out to retirement, pushing forms and administering a sympathetic ear to those whose lives had fallen apart—or being able to veer slightly off the margins. Nothing spectacular, nothing that her parents would ever be ashamed of, but if it meant results, if it meant just a small element of danger…

Two inspectors, two very different men, both dedicated to the job; one rigid, forthright, a credit to Malta and the islands, a regular by-the-book kind of man; the other, she liked. He hung around, and she suspected he was a bit dirty, or had been in his younger days. He certainly knew some interesting, one might say dubious, people, but he got results. He kept his ear not just to the ground but under the drains; he was prepared to get his hands more than dirty, willing, eager almost, to wipe the blood off with a damp sponge in the middle of Paceville if it meant nobody else stepped out of line. That's not to say he wouldn't let some things slide. "Pick your battles," he told me on my second day on the island. Pick your battles—maybe that's why he liked hanging around the doctor.

The diary interested him. It had more than piqued his curiosity, and it excited me to see the connection in his mind. This had been a long-play game, two people murdered—three if we include the doctor's mother—cool and calculated. The story of this act was more than just a whim; it was the end game of a long-held grudge, something rather poetic that the doctor might appreciate, if he were to survive.

They say we are never more than six degrees of separation from knowing someone. I found that statement ludicrous until my second year at university. With more than seven billion people in the world, how is that even possible? When my father was a young man, there weren't even three billion all scrambling for food and water, for life to have some meaning. Look at Malta at the same time: just over a quarter of a million people inhabit this jewel in the middle the sea, caught on all sides by people wanting to claim it, to protect it, to destroy it. They cannot all be bound by a degree of separation, a parlour game, a trick of population, and yet seemingly they are. They talk of families who survived the night during the darkest days of Nazi and fascist Italy's relentless bombings, of those who grew the best potatoes, those who were found to be womanisers, the fallen women and gambling addicts, and those who, by a single degree of that parlour trick, had been involved with both a policeman and a man of poetry.

In my second year of university, I got to meet a man quite a bit older than me but still good fun, who had made his way back to education after many years of travelling and occasionally pausing to reflect on a beach somewhere. Good fun, fallen on hard times, but he'd stuck out in his earnestness to achieve a degree. It didn't matter what level or attainment; he just wanted to say finally he had a bachelor of arts degree to his name. One evening, when most of the crew had gone home, he fished out his phone and said he wanted to show me a couple of pictures…in private.

I did not take him for a dirty old man, but perhaps we all harbour a secret desire or two. I was about to gently but firmly suggest he keep his thoughts purely platonic when I looked down at the first photograph and recognised one of the two men shaking hands. I looked up at him and smiled. The photograph was crude but certainly genuine, and I asked him why he carried a picture of John F. Kennedy on his phone. He looked me in the eye and told me he greatly admired the man, he would have given anything to meet him, and yes, he knew Kennedy had his dark side but he was a true leader, born for the job.

I was about to ask him about the young man shaking his hand, but before I could, he asked to shake mine. He smiled, and I laughed with genuine positivity in my heart. I reached out, gave him a true handshake of friendship and kept smiling…only hesitating when he proclaimed that now I had shaken the hand of someone who had shaken the hand of JFK.

His eyes twinkled, not out of jest or dishonesty but out of true faith that I would believe him. I knew right there and then he was telling the truth, but I still had to ask him how.

The young man in the picture was former president Bill Clinton, another great man in my heart—again, one whose dick perhaps did a lot more for relations than he could, but still a great man of history. He paused as I looked down at the photograph magnified on the screen. He didn't wait for me to ask; he shuffled on to the next picture on his phone and showed an almost magisterial Bill Clinton around the time of his 1992 election win. In the picture was, once more, a young man shaking a president's hand and smiling, not as choreographed as the first but still one taken in history's bright glare.

"It was taken not long before the election, when Clinton was at a rally, a meet-and-greet in New York. My friend and I took the afternoon to go down and listen though neither of us could vote, both what they call illegal. Both, if caught, would have been sent home. Still, you only get to meet a president once, don't you?"

I could not believe my eyes. Here was a middle-aged man in a back street public house, a man who had travelled but who now lived in a one-bedroom flat surrounded by dusty memories and the books he needed to make it through the demanding English course. A man educated by the world but whose knowledge of literature was confined to those he had found the time to read—mostly porn—as he bumbled through life. This was a man who had shaken the hand of President Clinton, who, in turn, had shaken the hand of President Kennedy. In that moment, I believed in the six degrees, but he wasn't finished and neither were the surprises.

He looked me in the eye and told me he had shown me those pictures because he wanted me to know he would never lie to me, that what he was going to show and tell me next might hurt, but he would not lie. I nodded; there was nothing else I could do. I told him to continue, realising that I now had a link with history and perhaps a microbe had escaped unharmed down through the generations and was now on my own Dutch hand; Kennedy's last breath in my possession.

He started talking about my family. He had known them when my father and mother were younger, and he again showed me a photograph, a bit blurred but most certainly of them and with him. They were at a party in a room somewhere…my grandmother's home. There was my aunt, my mother's sister—about the age I was at that moment, sitting in the pub.

It seems he was working in Amsterdam at the time. He'd got into trouble and was paying off his debt. A wrong turn, he said, the only one, but he paid for it. Six months in prison and then released, a minor issue by today's standards. He was befriended by my mother and father in the hope he would talk to my aunt about the dangers of drugs, of falling into the habit.

He looked at me sadly. My aunt had died before I was born, but I knew this to be true. He didn't have to explain. I believed him. He had no reason to lie, no need to make himself seem important; he had just lived on the road, stopping here and there, but he said he was very fond of my aunt, that he just could not stop her from falling. He blamed himself but knew there was nothing he could do when she met the man who took her life by forcing her to carry heroin in bags in her stomach. They lost touch, he could not bring himself to be around my father and mother anymore, and whilst they didn't hate him, they knew he had to leave.

As I watch, appearing disinterested in the clothes on the mid-price rail, I seek solace from my friend from university. I seek solace in the retribution and revenge the six degrees of separation can bring. I learned that day that you come into contact with people for a reason; they are there to show you what happened before and what could happen in the future. Six degrees... If I had not met my friend, I would never have seen that photograph. I would never have known that teaching was not for me. I would never have joined the police or met the inspector, never have read that diary and would not now be tailing a man who was in a photograph with my mother and father, my aunt and my friend from university. This was the degree of separation my friend had warned me about. Everything happens for a reason.

Two weeks after that conversation in the pub, another random moment occurred—one that makes complete sense now. My friend asked me to accompany him to an outside lecture as he was under the weather and needed help to get home should it get too much. I was free, I was intrigued about the talk, and it was a coup to get a ticket for such an event. It had been the talk of the English department for weeks; many of those on the course could not get a ticket. Some begged, borrowed and would have considered stealing from a close mate had the opportunity arisen. The famed poet, a man of letters, was coming to town for a one-off appearance to garner funds for the department and as a personal favour to one of the heads who had studied under him for a year.

Nothing in life is coincidence. I asked for the secondment to Malta, I searched ruthlessly for that diary, and I knew that the inspector would ask me to do some undercover work for him, strictly under the radar. Nothing is coincidence, but perhaps whether it falls into place is all on the spin of the dice.

He looked ill that day. They blamed it on jet lag, on not being used to the fish-and-chip supper they had plied him with. They joked with the crowd and attendees, and to be fair, he gave such a rousing performance he should have been on the stage himself. He would have made a magnificent Macbeth.

He held the audience in the palm of his hand, and my friend was in awe; I don't think he had heard or read much poetry before attending the classes and lectures, but he was in the grip of mania, his own health soon forgotten. All he wanted to do was listen to the words flowing out of the man's mouth and revel in his own discovery of learning. I thought he was OK, not brilliant—psychologically scarred, I mused at the time, not realising how correct I was.

At the end, the doctor signed autographs of his latest book, only for those who attended the lecture. He had kept the numbers to the barest minimum, he said. Aside from the fish and chips, he was not making anything from this small favour. He also didn't like large crowds, of that I was sure, as his eyes kept darting everywhere. They would not hold still, and whilst my friend believed he was searching for something, some recognition in a person's soul of their true love for the power of a sonnet, I reasoned he was making sure there was not a face in the crowd that might belong to the past.

The quarry is on the move. He is slick-haired and dressed in fine clothes; I notice a ring on his right index finger. I recognise the design. It used to belong to the doctor—I was sure it was his—a piece of jewellery he reported missing from the apartment he once shared with a now dead woman. The air of confidence is arousing. I would be remiss and neglectful to not admit that, but he is not a man to mess with. Two people had died at his hands in the last week, a third perhaps with my aunt. How many more lives? I understood the inspector's assertion that this was not revenge on the doctor for his past life away from the island, even as he sat at home and brooded over his own sins which led him here. This was about revenge for a long-since distant plea to a young friend to talk to the police about drugs that made their way to the island. Another time, another place, but still one filled with pure revenge.

I followed him. I was sure he had not seen me, but with the hand-wringing of experience, I soon realised he had given me the slip. Had he made me? Had he watched me as I had watched him? I retraced my steps in my mind and countered; no. There was no way he could have spotted me. I walked over to the takeaway café and ordered a coffee from the hatch. Finding no spare table, I was starting to rue my luck, when a small boy approached me with trepidation.

He handed me a piece of paper and waited for a coin or two. I didn't like to encourage such behaviour but thought in this circumstance that I should. He went away happy, and as I unfolded the scrawled note underneath the Maltese sunshine and surrounded by summer visitors, I found I was looking at a declaration of war.

11.

The Detective's Tale: A Meeting on the Howl

I SAW THE BEST *minds of my generation destroyed by madness.*" I had stared at the spray-painted graffiti at the bottom of the slope that ran into Triq It-Torri and Triq Gorg Borg Oliver many times over the years. At first, I believed it to be a symbol of wanton vandalism that would become endemic if we allowed it to spread. I had seen pictures on walls before, some of them ghoulish, some of them admittedly classy and filled with artistic temperament; it still did not mean I wanted the island to become a mural for those who couldn't get into an art school.

It wasn't until I coaxed the doctor down to St. Julian's Bay one evening after lectures that I took in another viewpoint. To say he was thrilled is to underestimate the emotion of the man and his love of such anarchy; to say he wept awhile is to suggest he was overcome, but he cried, he said, because whoever decided at that moment to take the words of Ginsberg and plant them in spray-painted anguish was either a genius or the most tortured of souls. I stood beside him at the bottom of that slope, taking in the first line from 'Howl', and believed I truly understood, for the first time, the man I had known for most of my life.

He was not commenting on the why, but on the very fabric of our time, where a fool can become leader of the free world, where nuclear warfare is talked up and lauded as the only way to deal with a problem and those who believe otherwise are considered unthinking, unpatriotic, walking time bombs who don't get the programme of events set out by those whose three-thousand-dollar suits mark them as anointed by God to issue a decree.

His face was haunted, and out of kindness and compassion, I put my hand on his shoulder. He cried some more. In between sobs and rolling tears, I heard him mention a girl's name, one unknown to me, so I left it there. It was a private grief, an unintentional name drop, and I should not have been privileged to hear it, not then, not in amongst the tears of remorse, not in the frustration he was enduring.

It was funny in retrospect. I was looking at those words as if they meant something to me, something more than the graffiti and statement. I was reminded of a track by a British progressive rock act in which the narrator says his head is haunted and he has become a ghost, an invisible man, an insubstantial moment with access to all the letters you have written. In that moment, here on my island, at the bottom of a slope bearing the words of a master of his art, with the dying light glaring off the crumbling incline, I waited for a man to show his face. I waited to read his letters and to hear the scream again, the Howl of the mad.

I forced myself to turn away from the words and looked across the bay at the bright lights, the sense of calm amongst the chaos. There was a killer close by, and whilst I believed I knew who it was, I could have been mistaken. So many mistakes made in my life, so many opportunities to make it right, all blown away on the edge of Winter's breath as it spat out Autumn's reverence.

On the other side of the road stood my Dutch colleague, arms folded, a steel-like gaze, sharp eyes reflecting the headlights of cars and buses as they rounded the top of the curve far too fast, spoiling their view and charm of St. Julian's Bay. I only ever hoped they slowed down enough to be enamoured by the sight of

Spinola Bay, or at least wouldn't crash on that hairpin bend just past the pharmacy.

She had called me as soon as she took in the gravity of the note handed to her by that small child. She of course recorded what he looked like so we could question him, but he could have been anybody's kid, all sticky and requesting more sweets, a child on holiday promised a couple of euros if he took this love letter over to the nice lady looking at the sunglasses stand.

I had intended to make sure my friend was safe all night, but after requesting one more officer to come to his house and sit with him, I felt sure that even if someone was to get past the two men on the gate, they would not get past an armed man with orders to shoot on sight…I hoped.

The letter was explicit; it mentioned both the doctor and me by name and was addressed, surprisingly, to my Dutch colleague by her first name. She seemed nonplussed, suggesting that whoever he was, he had certainly done his homework on the team.

I knew instantly the name signed at the bottom of the note, the flourish of the signature, almost autograph-like. My past had caught up with me, and I had to stare the Devil in the eye. My past—my part in a heroin deal gone sour, revived in time to see the errors of my ways and what I had already done wiped away like a sponge on a dirty plate, the trouble being, leave a plate too long drying on the side and you eventually see a smear, a shine, a mark which taunts your ability to do even the simplest of jobs without leaving a single trace of what was there.

I was a young boy. The farmer should not have been involved, but there were guns on his property. I wanted to steal them; instead, I saw what he had been hiding was far worse. I knew about drugs—about heroin—only from television police dramas and from knowledge of my father's work. I had also met a girl on one of the beaches once. She was gaunt, underfed, her arms betraying signs of abuse, bruises, marks, her own dinner plate tarnished with the residue of her life. I had pointed her out to the boy who would become my life-long friend, and his advice had been to steer clear because she looked like trouble.

All the while I searched my memory, I felt my colleague's eyes burn into my soul. She wanted answers—what could I say? Nothing that would allay the sense of trepidation rising in both of us. My island was under attack again, this time not from above, not from the skies, not from bombs dropped from planes bearing the Swastika. This was not about control under the jackboot and tyranny. This was about a market, pure forces of capitalism, supply and demand, getting a foothold in a foreign market, export and import, give the consumers what they need, a fair price, and do it all on the phone, the modern gateway drug. I wished I could have wept. I wished I could have phoned my father, brought the old chief out of retirement and given him the case; he would have no problem summoning up the courage to do what needed to be done next.

The laughter from Paul's Sea Breeze restaurant was loud and boisterous, a football match in progress on the owner's television, no doubt, only drowned out by the sound of the sea hurling itself against the wall. The clock was ticking. He would be here soon; the letter—short, polite, full of hidden menace—told me to be at the bottom of the slope for nine o'clock.

The type of cheer that indicated either a goal had been scored or the owner had offered free drinks thundered in rage against the noise of the sea. I smiled, knowing which one it would be. Then, from behind me, the noise of a car broke my hopeful reverie. Almost silent, almost deadly…too many people met their end this way. It had become a weapon in a war nobody truly understood. Take away our ability to maim somebody with a gun, we shall instead break their bones with the fender of a high-speed vehicle. I didn't understand it myself, but I was only a policeman.

Slowly, it crept down the hillside, its lights on full beam blinding me to the point of having to raise my left hand to my eyes, my right hand in my pocket, fingers poised to pull the trigger of my police issue gun. I could easily dive out the way; at the speed it was going, I could have walked up to the door, opened it, shot point-blank into the son of a bitch's face and claimed a moral victory. Of course, I would go to jail, or at the very least be run off the island when certain facts came to light.

The car rolled to a stop but kept its engines running, the slow growl, the panther stalking its prey. I thought of my colleague by the rails on the other side of the road. How much could she see? Could she see beyond the outline of the shadow? Did I look to her as if I were waiting for an invitation from God to join him in eternal boredom as the light beckoned me towards it? If not the haunting light made graceful by the poets then perhaps the naturalists—the lepidopterists who studied moths at night and their habit of hurling themselves into an electric grid believing it to be the hanging moon—would argue I was moth made human. My senses urged me to my destruction, my charred wings fluttering with singed ambition to reach that judgemental moon.

In my ear, I heard the breathing of the woman I was beginning to rely on heavily, loyal in many ways, secretive, yes, but damned good at her job. Her breaths matched my own; I felt exhilaration but also fear. Why had he stopped? What was he waiting for? The engine was still running, and I was braced to quickly jump out of the way. I did not want to join the spray-painted madness just yet. The bells of Knisja tal-Karmnu struck nine: right on time, then, if he was planning on taking me out here in St. Julian's Bay.

Still the car didn't move. Eventually, the engine stopped running and the bright light that had slaughtered and teased this human moth suddenly shut off. The moon had disappeared behind a cloud, not an insect to be seen. Nothing moved; the only sounds were that of my companion in the darkness asking me what was happening, the crash of the waves and a groan from the football spectators; an equaliser, perhaps.

Other cars may have gone by, buses certainly would have sped past on their way to Paceville and beyond. I cared not for them; I cared only for those things I cared about. Who wouldn't rather be enjoying the company of friends down by the sea's edge, cracking open a bottle of wine, joking, laughing at the world, talking earnestly of the day's events and half paying attention to the match taking place in some corner of Europe?

My colleague again asked me what was going on. I had no way of showing my concern that this was somehow a setup; at any second, another car would come off Triq It-Torri and speed up behind me. Caught between the two worlds, dying between two cars—what a way to go, in a threesome of metal and flesh, screwed from the front, taken from behind. Not my idea of a night out with friends and family.

I was tired of waiting and signalled discreetly with my now free left hand. Five metres separated us as I began to walk gingerly towards the car. It was unkempt, shabby, a bald patch on the nearside front tyre, rust spots, a badly neglected runaround. It was not what I was expecting. If this were his weapon of choice then he had come down in the world very hard. Even time in prison did not make someone of his standing relish being chauffeured in a car you could buy for a couple of hundred euros and would be better of lying down in a scrapyard and begging to be put out of its misery. It was a wreck, a disaster of a vehicle.

Something was not right. My gut-ache told me so, and I heard Dutch in my earpiece. She was swearing with such ferocity. I made my way to the driver's side; through the glass, I could see the figure of a young man, his hands on the wheel, and he was visibly shaking. His nerves became more acute as I slowly drew out my gun and pointed it at his head.

My own nerves were betraying me. I would not normally act that way; I had only pulled the trigger twice in all my time on the police force, and both were in self-defence. I stepped back slightly from the door and violently tugged out my earpiece, never once taking my eyes off the young driver, never once lowering my gun. I issued a warning but with no effect; I shouted the instruction to get out of the car and identify himself. Still he was unforthcoming. It looked like he was carrying out instructions that had already been given to him.

Minutes had passed since the bells of the old Carmelite Church had sounded. I had been slow to resolve the situation; this was against all my training. I should have secured the site and got the driver out of the car immediately. Instead, I had waited nearly ten minutes to get this far.

I heard my colleague shout to me, "Fire!"

What fire? I wasn't going to shoot the boy in the car! I just wanted to scare him as he had unnerved me.

Slowly, he turned his head towards me and gestured that he was going to come out, mouthing, "Don't shoot. Please don't shoot." He got out of the car as though any sudden movement would seriously hamper his ability to produce an alibi for his innocence.

He closed the door with his backside and put his hands back in the air, a defeated man acknowledging just how much he was going to suffer, playing it cool but his body language said he was terrified.

I shouted out to him, "What is the meaning of this?" I had been expecting someone else, someone much more advanced in age, someone with whom I once had a connection. He smiled and replied, matter of fact, that he had a message for me from an old friend. I nearly jumped ten feet in the air as a heavy hand clamped down on my shoulders. It was a wonder the gun didn't go off, but if it had, it would have been drowned out by the quarter of bells that began to chime.

My partner shouted at me again. "Fire!"

Again, what fire? I got her to slow down. She growled I should have kept my earpiece in. We had been set up; this was not the grand stand-off, the inquisition I had dreamed of. This was but a double deal.

She kept talking. All the while, I kept watching the young driver for any sudden movements as he explained. His boat was on fire—the doctor's boat was on fire on the other side of Valletta.

"Didn't he sell it?" I asked. I was sure he told me he had sold it a few days ago—the day I told him his mother was dead. I stared at the boy hard, my anger rising. I moved towards him, and in a show of petulance and police-driven irritability, I placed the gun under his chin and demanded he tell me what the message was.

He was calm now, any sign of distress having fluttered away in the breeze. He waited for the final chime of the church bells before he spoke just one word. His eyes remained fixed and his gaze hardened, but I saw with dismay that his pupils were dilated—piss holes in the snow, my father used to say. Confidence courtesy of a narcotic; which one, I didn't know. All I wanted was the message. He leant forward, my gun muzzle pressing deeper into his neck, and whispered into my ear the word. *Boom.*

12.

A Tale of Duplicity: The Fire and the Detective

I WAS NEVER ONE for celebrating Guy Fawkes Night. Thankfully, it wasn't very popular on the island when I was a boy. Not enough Brits lived there to either make a big deal of it or perhaps make a mockery of a Catholic hero, and I only ever witnessed it once as a teenager. My father had taken my mother and me to London as part of an educational trip, a chance to learn about the wider European thought, he declared, to see for ourselves the memorial dedicated to the island and located near the Tower of London. It was an exciting moment, one filled with trepidation for my parents as they were also looking for clues to what may have happened to my grandfather.

I wasn't aware of that until much later. All I knew at the time was that this was a couple of days of newly found independence, of being trusted to behave myself on my own for a few hours in a large capital city. It was heaven and hell in one giant combination, a bonfire that, if respected, would be seen as a signal, a lantern of the onset of the best years of my life and the lie of university; although not truly academically minded, my father was sure I was able to attend on a scholarship—to do anything other than acquaint myself with his work and become a policeman, pounding the beat, keeping the peace or becoming embroiled in local politics. To him, even criminality had a nobler stance in life than the shady deals of high office.

My sister had cried off. The thought of even going across water, let alone swimming in it, was too much for her, and my parents worried for her future. What can an islander do if she will not dip her toe in the sea, float along on her back and look to the sky, to the plane overhead that would take her to parts unknown? I would never get to the bottom of her phobia of the water; her diary only gave small clues. I tried to ask her outright once; it was a couple of weeks before she drowned. She simply shrugged, her shoulders rising sharply the one time before she made her excuses and left the dining room where I had reluctantly broached the subject.

I witnessed my first bonfire in London, but I was to feel the flame and heat of that night for many years. It was the moment where shame first arose, and to this day is one I managed to keep from my father.

I sat down, more like crumpled in desperation, on the police car seat, the upholstery starting to smell of the remains of a burning yacht that somehow had not infected, with its dying sounds and acrid explosion, more than two other smaller boats in the marina. A bonfire of vanity, my friend would have called it. Myself and the driver were pushed back to a safe distance and, like those who had seen the fire from the Three Cities—no doubt watching through windows along the road, a glass and asphalt moat between sea and the small capital, and who may have silently cheered as one of the signs of ostentation in the built-up harbour cracked, creaked and sent noxious smoke into the air—may have considered catching a ferry sometime soon to go and see a real display of smoke and plumes of acidity and fire at Etna, a more distinctive force of nature.

I had sent my colleague straight to the doctor's house, to make a further check on him and see what sort of light he could add to the blazing fire being tackled by a company of brave men. The mast caught last, a fitting end; no lookout on top, no icebergs to navigate past; only rocks, strewn in the path of both the lecturer of English and me. We had so much that bound us together. On reading the diary of my late wife, her references to past events, her allusions to the whole sorry mess she'd helped cause if not instigated, I was surprised our pasts had not caught up with us before, that death in the form of a devil, an imp, a master of the art of deceiving, had not dealt revenge on us. Why wait until we were the age we were now?

I took my mobile phone out of my pocket and rang through to Control, bypassing the radio completely. Some conversations you don't have in public, if possible. I asked them to ring anyone in authority at Scotland Yard and find out when my suspect had been released from prison. I believed not that long ago—a few short months, perhaps—just enough time to get everything into place.

My driver had been busy. Whilst I'd watched this bonfire crackle and whine in the dark, he'd found the three men whose boats had been closest to the doctor's yacht and questioned them. Voluntarily, they came over to talk to me. They knew they had not only had a close call with their own pride and joy, paid for on the back of whispered allegations, short-changed deals and the eagerness of embracing a culture that really should have burned out long ago, but had got away with their lives by being quick, efficient and not asking a single question.

Each had received a phone call at eight o'clock that night; each had heard the same man give them instructions to move their vessels by 8:50 p.m. unless they wanted to see their investment go up in smoke. None of the three men wasted time, all arriving by 8:30 p.m. and all either out in the wider bay or safely moored in a different dock.

The Three Cities area buzzed with excitement. A crowd had gathered behind us, and I suspected many of them would have felt more at home watching football somewhere on the island. As I listened to the three men's almost exact and unsurprising stories,

I felt as if everybody had crawled from behind their doors and seen the spectacle escalate. From Birgu to Senglea and Cospicua, I imagined front doors being opened and relocked, scurrying feet rushing to get a good vantage point—in my cynicism, I half supposed an ice cream van might come along on the off-chance of making a killing as the spectacle grew to its finale. Why not? It was only natural for people to make money at such a time.

My first bonfire—my first large-scale fire—I watched with interest in a park close to the hotel we'd stayed in, the sense of the historic just a few yards away as the night sky tried but failed majestically to envelop the home of kings and queens, of the dear departed and of characters from history books. My father had told me that a relative of ours had met his end on the other side of the road during the War of the Three Kingdoms when he'd attempted, treasonously, to sell land he had captured for the soon-to-be-beheaded king and given it to Cromwell. Of course, that type of backhanded deviousness never works; it sets a stain down through the generations. When pressed, my mother told him to stop teasing me, and yet something in his manner, his raised eyebrow, suggested that the truth was not so far from the guesswork ventured.

Whilst my parents had gone for dinner and theatre—something starring a big name, a real force and presence on the stage—I was happily watching the shadows on the wall dance with delight and no care; shamanistic, silhouette, insubstantial puppets flickering in and out of existence. This was poetry for me, the dance of the wild and the historic. We had history on Malta; it was all around us. It was deep in the tunnels where our grandparents had sheltered as the bombing raids intensified. In the remains of the George Cross, they huddled together, and in the moments between, they prayed to God to save them from obliteration.

I had only been to London a few times in my life, but each time I went, I felt drawn to the East End, to the proud people who shared my island's horror, left scarred and disfigured by a government that didn't care about the ordinary man in Whitechapel or the average woman in Birgu.

I had walked the streets of Whitechapel with a keen eye when in London. I had noticed the area and those surrounding it were perhaps the most true part of the capital, the people, the lack of honour bestowed upon them by authorities, where danger lurked around every corner and where villains were lauded as kings. It was fitting that my first visit in the shadow of such downtrodden regal flair, my first brush with the wrong side of the law, had happened in plain view of the building which instilled terror. I should have run to Traitor's Gate and thrown myself into the water below.

I didn't place stock in coincidence; everything happens and everything is somehow connected. I knew people who couldn't see the connection, who saw A as being as different from Z as black is from white. The three men in front of me were all singing the same song. The tune was rehearsed, and I was sure the lyrics had been passed around and memorised. I didn't believe they could all have answered a call at eight p.m. and got down to the harbour in time. I wasn't even sure the boats they had moved were theirs.

All too convenient, all too tidy and placed into boxes for my delight. Was I supposed to ignore this coincidence? What about my friend? He had sold the boat. Why target something that no longer belonged to him? Wouldn't it be easier to torch his house, to shoot him, to break into his home and destroy every note and thought he had ever had?

To discredit him. That was it. Somehow, it came down to discrediting him and me together. We were bound in life as we would be in shame.

The girl, she'd known who the man was, the man who came up to her on the steps of the church in Liverpool. My ex-wife had known or, at least, guessed at his identity and gone along for the ride, not believing for a minute she would end up a casualty of a war that started in a park in London over thirty years before. My friend, he had surely never met him but had done his best to pull me out of a situation that would have put me six foot under by the time I was eighteen. Connections, a spider's web, started in the past and woven across decades, all with the intention of pulling us in, all designed intricately to make us dance on the streets of Malta for public consumption, and for revenge.

My phone rang. I asked the three gentlemen to be quiet for a moment and gave a discreet signal to the officer at my side to make ready with handcuffs. The voice on the other end of the line was alert, excitable. I had to get them to slow down and repeat it but this time louder. Over the sound of a final burst of flame and the crack of what remained of a charred hull, the yacht started to sink into the bay. There was an audible cheer from a section of onlookers, their night's entertainment worth the hurried dressing and pouring out of a couple of local bars. It was free, dynamic and best of all, some rich sod's nose had been knocked out of shape.

She repeated her statement, and then I knew for certain. All those burning embers, all the smoke and mirrors…it was just a game, a man out to create havoc and get revenge on two notable citizens, the two young men—two *boys*—who had crossed him.

I thanked the policewoman on the other end of the line and made a mental note to check up on her. I knew she'd had a few issues of late, some regarding advancement, some regarding a colleague.

I smiled at the three men, their bodies surrounded by the image of the last vestige of life, a halo of fire, as the yacht sank beneath the waves, the boat I had badgered my friend to let me experience. I would have dearly liked to sip a couple of beers as I watched the sea and sky shake hands then gently embrace, to chase the horizon, to push it back and watch it go on forever.

That horizon was permanently out of reach and yet clinging on, hopeful for a lingering touch.

I read the three men their rights. I had cause to believe they were not who they said they were; they were not being entirely truthful regarding the evening's events. As the constable placed handcuffs on two of the men, I grabbed the third by the scruff of his neck and without ceremony threw him against the side of the car. The loud bang startled a nearby couple, and I was amused. They had cheered and applauded the death knell of a maid of the sea without batting a single eyelid in surprise yet jumped almost a foot in the air at the sound of human skin and bone colliding with police car metal.

As I read the third man his rights, I noticed one of the couple regain their composure and make as if to start filming me, perhaps hoping for the peep show of assault, the chance to become the Kathryn Bigelow of the island. *Police officer physically attacks innocent man on quay side—buy tickets now.* I scowled and barked at them, in my best authoritative voice, that if they also wanted to be detained for the murder of two people then to carry on; they would have plenty of company in the cells.

The young couple thought better of it, and the woman urged the man to put his phone away and go home. I had never really been this rough before on someone, I had never really been the gruff, authoritarian type, and it was becoming a dangerous habit. Mercifully, I didn't draw my gun this time.

I called for a police patrol van to get down to the Three Cities and meet us as close to the Triq San Lawrenz as possible. I was stretching the resources at my disposal quite thinly, almost threadlike, but at some point this was going to end. The constables would go back to dealing with petty theft, harassed shopkeepers and all manner of complaints that a force had to deal with when tourists made their way to Malta in search of sun and escape.

My phone started to ring again; it was Dutch, and I clicked it off for a moment. Compared to what had been going on down here, my friend's troubles were trivial. He was guarded; he was safe. I, on the other hand, was feeling the pressure of the job and my life like never before.

I didn't like to ignore a call from a fellow officer, and by the time the constable and I had made two trips to Triq San Lawrenz and got all three prisoners into the wagon whilst urging people to make their way home—the show was now at the bottom of the marina until the wreck could be brought back to the surface to be investigated—she had called four more times. I was not in the mood.

I felt out of control. I had pulled my gun on a young lad who was quite obviously stoned, or worse. I had let my judgement slip in relation to many aspects of the case. Finally, I called Dutch back. She swore at me in her native language, and I realised that another ball had been dropped. In the background, I heard pandemonium, hell realising the cage door was unlocked. I asked as directly as I could what was going on. Was she all right? Had there been an attempt on the doctor's life?

The crash of a cabinet falling to the floor was jolting, and I heard her scream that whilst my memory was correct—the yacht had been sold privately—it seemed the good doctor had overlooked one tiny detail as he had made his plan to flee with a woman young enough to be his daughter.

Another scream, this time in absolute pain, and Dutch pleaded...something about a gun...he was holding a gun and was about to pull the trigger. A shout, the sound of a bullet being released from its chamber, a thud.

My mind raced. What had I unleashed tonight?

13.

A Tale of Three Guns

THERE IS NOTHING quite like an unexpected weapon suddenly positioned just a couple of inches from your head to make you alert and scared for your life. It is the true moment that hangs in the silence of the tick between the tock in which we see blackness and experience the microsecond of realisation that the world is over.

I watched him pull his gun on the driver of the car without hesitation. Not so much of a problem, easily contained, or so I thought at the time, but I should have recognised the signs. This was a man under considerable stress, and it seeped out of him like a poison. Slow and methodical instantly turned to rage. This man, who had built his reputation on the precise, on walking away and thinking the scenario through, was now a ticking bomb.

To be honest, I quite liked it. It showed passion, a willingness to fight for what was right, and yet it was shocking to see his gun go into that young man's face, pressed up against the sweat and the skin, demanding he answer to the highest authority on the island—his conscience—all for the sake of a stoned addict who had probably been given fifty euros and some coke to act as a decoy.

There is something intensely sexual about firing a gun and shooting someone. People think of it the wrong way; they see it as a murder weapon, one more to add to the list of ways a person can die at the hands of another—strangulation, poison, the accidents waiting to happen—it is a long list. We are a creative species. They see the bullet as the final moment, the sudden eclipse in the eyes, and yet murder is not about any of that. It is mostly about the sense of sexual arousal and passion, which is why murder is against the law. It means we, as animals, have to fuck each other's brains out every now and then in order to assert control.

Voltaire once said, 'It is forbidden to kill, therefore all murderers are punished unless they kill in large numbers and to the sound of trumpets.' Stalin, Hitler, Pol Pot…their names are infamous, rightly considered to be vile, shunned and left in the darkness, but they were lauded by millions. Did they ever pick up a gun outside of the battlefield? Did they kill with their own hands once they were in a suit and tie and shaking hands with other officials? If only Chamberlin had not been so blindsided, perhaps he could have taken a gun to Munich and pressed it against the Devil's head. Diplomacy straight out of the water, but it would have driven home the message: *Adolf, I like you. I wish to put a bullet in your filthy anti-Semitic mother-fucking brain. Now, open your mouth, darling, and take it like a man.*

I watched him from the other side of the road. The steady flow of traffic—steady enough, anyway, for the island—passed by in a blur. Through bus widows and over the top of car roofs, I saw him stand watching the car for what seemed an absolute age. He was caught between minds, between actions. That worried me an awful lot more than what was to follow; an indecisive officer was a dead one.

The reception by St. Julian's Bay had not been good all evening. It was with some surprise that I had even managed to get a text message saying there was a fire at the marina in the Three Cities area. It was hardly relevant to the case; probably just some drunken idiot who'd blown his life savings on a gambling table and taken it out on a boat somewhere, or an insurance job.

This is what happens when money becomes scarce; another sexual twist in the minds of some. If they cannot keep it, they fuck it up badly. It doesn't matter if it is a hotel, a super-size yacht, a nation or a person; if they don't want to deal with the responsibility of keeping it going, of making sure it is loved, then what do they do? They give it away, let someone else take on the job or splash petrol around and strike a match.

When I saw his gun go into the lad's neck, I knew I had to act. I didn't want this on my conscience. Yes, perhaps he deserved to be frightened a little. Perhaps he needed to be taken down before he'd impart what he knew, but it would have only taken a car to backfire somewhere behind him and rattle his nerves, and the slope would have seen a different perspective on how a policeman can take somebody's life.

Just as I realised I had to run across the road, another text came through, followed by the sound of several messages missed, my voicemail deciding I was an awful human being, and then the short, sharp buzz of a telephone call.

Instinctively, I knew it was our quarry, the man we were both chasing for very different reasons. He said hello in a very polite, British way and asked how I was. Was I still bitter about my aunt? She was, after all, just a drug-addled girl who had lost her own war and succumbed to want and peer pressure. He rebuked me for not having a better phone, one that could take the pressure of calls in an area where everybody was using up the limited bandwidth. If I had moved a little further from the buses at their stops, I would have got the message bang on nine p.m.

It would have been more fun that way—more dramatic, more a feel of a show. Now it was lost in time. The junkie would still say his lines, but he would not get the laugh from the audience he deserved. Before he hung up, he told me to ask the doctor if he had enjoyed counting his money yet. The yacht did not come cheap, after all.

My grandfather was a good man—kind, gentle, looked after his family and provided them with what he could after the end of World War Two. Money was tight, the area they lived in still bore the scars of occupation many years after the war had ended, but he had so much love to give.

He had his family late in life, a young man of twenty by the time the Germans walked through the Netherlands and Belgium on their way to Paris. He had vowed to not become romantically involved with anyone until he was sure that Nazism was banished forever. He lasted until 1967; love does not see the future. At the age of forty-eight, he found a woman to love, a survivor of Belsen, a young girl who had been saved by a British medic, who took life on the chin and made it her mission to survive whatever the cost. She told me once that she asked the medic to dance with her. Through his radio, which crackled and burned the ears when the wind was racing in the wrong direction, she'd felt the love of Gracie Fields coming across the air like a beautiful ghost. It was sound of freedom, of having been through all hate could throw against her and come out the other side, emancipated, thin, with the indignity of lice crawling in her hair and a group of men that wanted to kill her for every breath she stole from them.

She adored the medic, but soon she was shipped back to her home—all rubble and ash but still a point of beginnings—and slipped back into her old life. When she met my grandfather, he was already forty-eight, his time to become a father long since passed, gently easing into retirement and eventually evenings of wondering when the end may come. With our help, he kept going, not passing away until 2010 at a good ninety years of age. She was twelve years younger than him when they met, but she had never married. I like to believe it was because she was waiting for someone who looked and acted like the medic from Britain, the young soldier who had taught her to dance to Gracie Fields.

It was not easy, she said. Her story was known in her home town; her parents were both dead—lots of parents were killed, maimed, shot and disappeared during those dark days—and she was damaged property. When my grandfather turned up one day out of the blue and she saw him working on rebuilding the old synagogue, she knew somehow that it was him and nobody else.

I love stories like that. They give me hope, a reason to hang on to the world no matter what is pressed against me.

A gun should never reside in the hands of a civilian. It leads to destruction and accidents. Yet my grandfather had one in his shed, hidden away underneath a false flagstone. I found it one day, not completely by accident, as I had heard my mother talking about it to my father.

My grandfather was a private man. None of us really knew, until after he died, the full extent of his story, of his own fight against tyranny and the fight for freedom for his country. There had been whispers, of course, the odd rumour that kept him on edge when it found its way to his ears—nothing that would rattle the majority. I suspected, even at a young age, there was more to this man than blowing up railway lines and working secretly to overthrow the alleged New World Order.

Early police work…perhaps I was born nosy. I soon figured that if the story was to have any credence, then in his shed I would find proof. It made sense to the young girl that I was, on the back of war and terror, in the uncertainty of a nuclear strike in Europe. Where would you keep a weapon to aid your family and keep them out of further harm's way?

I found it on my next visit to my grandparents' home; my grandfather had been unwell for a while, the shock of losing a daughter still very raw in his head. He still went out every day and came back with his small blue book full of drawings and cryptic notes, but he wasn't the man he had been. Almost beaten, certainly bloodied, but still proud.

It wasn't that hard to find the gun. Underneath his workbench was a stone that was out of place, not sharing the uniformity of the others which looked as though they could do with a scrub as years of iron filings and shaved-down wood had left their mark, their tattoo on the floor. I lifted it up, expecting it to be heavy and difficult to budge, but to my surprise it came away easily. It was a thin piece of stone, barely a few millimetres thick, underneath it a small hole dug into the earth, just big enough to hold a six-inch-high tin. I breathed heavily; a secret uncovered. I could have put it back straightaway, my curiosity partly sated; I knew something my mother and father didn't.

But I got sloppy. My eager, questioning young mind took hold above reason. I opened the tin and inside found a red cloth, clean, cared for. I put the tin on the floor beside me and gently took the cloth and its heavy load out. Unfolding the cloth, I came across, what I learned later, was a German Luger. So transfixed was I, that I didn't hear the back gate swing open. I paid no attention to the sound of footsteps coming down the path, and until the door swung open and I saw my grandfather's face contorted in an ugly mix of rage and despair, I honestly believed I was going to get away with my childish investigation.

What had I expected? For him to sit down and tell me why he had hidden a German gun in his shed? For us to bond over a tale or two of his heroism? To be inspired and see him as the hero of Dutch resistance? If I did then I was stupid, a fool, a nosy little girl who deserved a spanking, one from my grandfather and then one from my father.

He shouted, a mixture of regret, annoyance, outright shame, disgust, Dutch and a few choice words he had picked up from my grandmother over the years. He slammed his fist against the wooden structure and only stopped when, exhausted, he saw me cowering beneath the workbench. I didn't mind the punishment to come, but I truly didn't want to be hit, to feel the back of a hand or indeed a punch in the face. I had seen that happen to my aunt not long before she died. It looked painful; it looked degrading.

He sank to his knees and started to cry, but his tears were not for me. They were for himself. I think, now, I had broken him, invaded the last remaining piece of him that had stood firm since the war. Not even my aunt's death at the hands of heroin had pinpricked that mighty resolve. He grabbed the gun with both hands and, placing it against his temple, closed his eyes and raged again, asking me to shoot, to take away the pain, saying he would never blame me in death. All the sins he had committed, the sacrifices he had chosen between, he no longer wanted them in his head. He urged me to pull the trigger. "Blow them to hell, little one," he said in English.

There is nothing worse in life than seeing an old man broken. When a woman is taken that far, people rally round. They care. When a man does it, he is seen as weak, a pathetic ghost.

Slowly, I let go of the gun and left him holding it between his palms. I asked him gently how many people he had killed during the war. Realising he was now the only one holding the gun, he carefully drew it away from his temple, and through tears, he gave me an answer that still makes my skin crawl to this day.

He put the gun back inside the tin, the red cloth once more wrapped tightly around it, but instead of putting it back in the hole and disguising it with the thin slab, he put it in the left pocket of his grey mackintosh coat. I had broken him, but in a way, I had made him less afraid. In the simple act of wishing for his life to be over, I had absolved him of the need to have the weapon anymore.

His words to me resonated across the invisible thread binding that moment to this. The doctor with a gun in his hand; a bullet already fired and tearing a hole through the middle of a large, black-covered book before embedding itself in the study wall; the gun now up against my head. It was a mirror of what had happened long ago.

Sweat poured off his brow, along with the smell of intoxicating fear, as he raged about money, about being cheated. Had I known? Of course I had known; his friend had known. He had blown everything on a simple wish to get out of the country, to start again with a woman he actually liked, and in a moment of weakness, he had become so blind, so greedy, he never checked the money he received for the yacht; not until I reminded him to do so.

He dropped his guard, the strain becoming too much for him, probably not thinking I would fight back. I had every sympathy for him, but I was not going to die at the hands of someone who saw only words and shadows in his mind.

I punched him hard and fast in the gut, and he fell to the floor. With a single move, I made it to the door and got my phone out to call the inspector. A second shot rang out and the wooden frame splintered. He went to fire again, but as I cried out for help, I heard a click, and another, a fast beat of empty chamber and dust. I stopped and looked at the man who had held students in the palm of his hand with a simple phrase and realised he was, now, like my grandfather: broken.

Always be wary. Be afraid of the man who, when asked how many men he has killed with the pistol in his quivering hands, has to think before answering with the words, *I lost count.* Take pity on the man who, when asked the same question whilst holding a gun, answers with downcast eyes and a lump in his throat, *none.*

14.

The Farmer's Statement: 1987

I WAS GOING BROKE. No savings, no government backing, mortgaged beyond all possibility of digging myself out of the debt I had gotten into by trying to keep my family afloat and the ghosts of the past appeased by working on a farm that was doomed from the moment my grandfather died. You tell me—would you have not grabbed the olive branch? Wouldn't you have flirted with hope if it meant you could eat, that your children would have clothes? Of course heroin is evil, but so is starving to death when the government is not doing a single thing to help you survive.

It's easy to make a decision about the moral stance you would take when it does not involve you personally, when you are the one not affected by the outcome. You see it every day, hear about someone's problems, the choice they have to make between A and B, the agony of letting someone down or following their heart, moving away from family in the pursuit of their dreams, or the simple things like white bread or brown...whether to sleep with the boy even though, at fourteen, it could mean jail or pregnancy. All these problems of the everyday—they are what make us tick, are they not? Well, what made me tick was the survival of the family farm.

I know you're not going to tell me, but how long have I been under surveillance? I don't believe it was for very long—I can almost guess the date because I'm sure it was the night when I saw a prowler creeping around the farm. A figure, a shadow, a sprite going after either the guns that had been locked down in one of the barns or the shipment I had collected from Marsaxlokk the previous day. I tried to capture the person—I would have broken their neck—but they were too agile for me. They could have only been young, and slippery, treacherous, like all young folk these days. I've seen television; I've seen and read the reports of them being irresponsible, taking up drugs to see the world in a different way, to rebel against the past…bastards, all of them. So if they want to get out of their minds, who am I to argue? It was money to keep my farm afloat. Let them take as much heroin as the supplier leaves in my barn. Let them rot for all I care.

No, I never touched the stuff myself. Don't want to know. I've seen addictive personalities before. My father was a gambler, you see. He thought it was a more worthwhile pursuit than growing crops. Building a reputation as a good farmer was beyond him—could not see even the winning post all that often as he spent more time down at the racing track amongst horses than he did picking potatoes. An addict is an addict is an addict, my grandfather would often say to me—didn't matter if it was wine, food, horses or drugs. If it got you, if you could not imagine a day when you would not think about it, without craving the taste, without seeing the next big win at the track, then you were an addict.

Simplicity, it was all I ever wanted. I believed, like my grandfather, that from good hard work, from being honest with your neighbour, respecting the boundaries that have been part of Maltese life for generations and looking after the family, then you had everything you could hope for. Life was simple and affirming. We believed that. My grandmother believed it, too, before her life was cut short by the hangover of war—it was a shame that my father didn't have the same outlook. He was the thrill seeker, the tearaway, the gambling man, the one who broke us. I just happened, in the end, to realise that the body of the farm was beyond saving and would be the one to bury it.

I'm a simple man—no need for poetry or books in my life. All I loved was the soil, its brown clumpy nature, the feel of it as it sifted between my fingers, the end result a thousand bags at a time, packed and sent to market or even across the water. A simple man whose father started lining up debts across the country.

On the night my grandfather died—content, happy that he had at least one relative who would see the farm through to the twenty-first century and keep it in the family name—my father achieved notoriety by placing the farm down as collateral on a bet in the UK. A big race, a sure thing—he believed that with his whole heart. Even when he paid the heavy price for his addiction, I did not shed a tear because he left me with the choice of letting the farm go and seeing my grandfather's work go to waste or taking out a loan to cover his bet. What choice did I have? You say potato, I say potato.

If I could dig up my father's body now, I would probably do so and chop off what remains of his head, the decomposed skull with worms and beetles feeding on what is left of skin and muscle. I would hammer it to pieces, smash it into the smallest of fragments, and then I would smile broadly. I would smile for the pain that man caused. There are parents, loved ones, friends of those who die because of the addiction I have helped fuel. In my mind, though, my actions were born of circumstance; his, that no good weasel of a man, were born of greed.

I ask you, whose was the greater crime?

Was it mine? Am I the one whose life was ruled by addiction? Was I the one who pitted the family livelihood against the possibility of a horse coming in first in a race hundreds of miles away? No! Have I fuelled an addiction in others? Well, I will let the courts decide that. You will press charges, the media will have a field day, but in time, I will be forgotten. I will have a semblance of life that I did not have whilst my father was alive and destroying what was rightfully mine.

I was relieved the day he took his life. A gunshot to the head, blood splattered all over the back wall of the barn, a sentence delivered and executed in a brief moment of recognition of what he had done. His last minutes were not spent pleading for his life; no panel of twelve good men and true, no lawyer present, no defence counsel, the only witness was me. I said nothing. I let him talk; I let him ramble for a while; I let him pull the chamber back, slide the barrel up to his mouth, place the butt of the rifle flat against the barn floor, and in one swift action, he was gone.

One minute, he was there, the flash in the pan, the big ideas man to whom betting was an all-consuming passion; the next, he was dead, the finished article, the empty hole exciting the senses of flies and worms.

I stood motionless for what seemed an eternity, the shock of it refusing to leave my eyes, the jolt of the unexpected hitting home. I was numb, not with the disbelief but with the sudden realisation of how much he'd actually cared. He'd wanted to save the family—his son, his daughter, wherever she was, and the grandchildren—the pain of a trial. He couldn't stop the papers going over the fine details of his habit and how much it had cost those around him, but he could save them from seeing his face ever again.

I stood there at the entrance of the barn, chewing over his final words, his declarations and intents, wondering what I could have said to him if there had been time, if I'd had the inclination.

I stood there frozen in the doorway, casting a shadow down the length of the barn, and, seeing it stop a few centimetres from where the gun now lay on the floor, the smoke fighting the shadow for supremacy, mixing and blending like a surreal painting, the colour drained, and all that was left was black and white, a scene of a world that would not leave my eyes.

I stood there long after I heard the sirens in the background, long after my daughter held my hand and urged me to walk away, to let the ambulance driver and the policemen do their work.

My wife had heard the gunshot. She'd seen me standing motionless. Like the vision of a mighty ship pulling into port in Valletta, the magnitude of the situation was more than enough to make you stop and stare with your mouth half open as the weight of life shifts.

Being watched by someone you know to be there but cannot see sends you into the world of nightmares. You constantly search for the signs, the whites in the eyes that reflect in the darkness, the noise you know should not be there, a small creak on the stairs when everybody else is asleep or wrapped gently in each other's arms whilst you try to keep the paranoia at bay. You arm yourself at night; you sit there in your rocking chair and feel each movement, forwards, backwards, forwards, backwards. You look into the dark, look for life, knowing full well that the shadow is staring straight back at you, and it is hungry.

There are always signs. I started placing in the gorses, and obvious hiding places, old rusty animal traps that I found in one of the smaller barns, hidden away under years of neglect and dust and decay. Old tractor parts had covered them up, and they had become interlocked, terrifying in their monstrosity, their barbaric nature. Perfect, I thought, to catch out the voyeur. I had studied over the course of a week the patterns in the dirt, in the straw I'd laid down to soak up the puddles where I'd created small indentations in the ground to see if footprints developed on their own—a wandering ghost, perhaps my father's, looking for somewhere to sleep that wasn't a furnace heated by hell—or if indeed it was my psyche taking offence at the evil I had let into the island. The evil I was sheltering, giving house room to before waving it goodbye with cold, hard cash placed in my hand in return.

I had never really wanted to change the farm much. I had ideas, of course, but on the whole, I wanted to keep it very much how it had been when my granddad had watched over it. I could have gotten rid of the bushes that surrounded the farm, but in my heart I knew they were as much of this place as I was. Trim them back but never destroy. I ran around these bushes when I was a child, playing soldiers, pirates, smugglers.

Soldiers die in battle; they lose limbs, they become the enemy and are booed and jeered by their countrymen. Pirates were romantic once; now they decimate the seas and bring people across from lands touched by the wars of those soldiers. It will get worse as the years go by, that much I know.

Smugglers are invisible; everybody despises them but cannot wait to see what has been brought ashore later appear in their living rooms, bedrooms and kitchens. The transportation of goods without paying excise duty is beneficial to them. They don't care what the repercussions are. Crates of Scotch whisky, a few hundred pounds of undocumented beef, radios, television sets, albums, videos, games, clothes, and tons of heroin; they all leave their mark on society.

Some get the chance to taste whisky they believe was bottled in one of the finest distilleries in the world when, in actual fact, the crew took it home and substituted it with a cheap knock-off made somewhere in the Far East, the trick being to put clear nail varnish around the cap and let it harden. When the customer, who has never tasted a whisky of such quality before, goes to open it, they hear the crack and assume it is the cap being pierced, its edge being torn clean.

Supply and demand: they get what they want—a drop of excellence—and the smuggler gets money to put away for the really big drop—human cargo, the brides for Western men, slaves, all as undocumented as the beef and the pork and lamb coming in and both sets of meat more than likely containing a disease that will rot away the guts and the soul.

Smugglers were treated with a bit more respect than the army. For every soldier who fought during World War Two, the psychological problems they came back with were many fold, but a smuggler doesn't bottle up his anger. If he's feeling the nerves, he consoles himself by adding an extra charge to the usual fee. Anything can be made better by earning an extra few hundred pounds for a single drop.

I didn't want to have the heroin here on the farm, but it made sense. Nobody suspected me. I didn't go flash with the money; I used it sparingly but wisely, slowly getting rid of a bill here and there, reducing my loans and being creative. Of course, the man who put all this into motion should take the credit: a well-spoken Englishman, pinstripe suit and fancy collar but prepared to get his hands dirty; organised enough that, should anyone cross him, they would feel his wrath sooner or later. He came up with a plan to harvest my potatoes quicker and found a market for them; suddenly my farm was making a profit again, more or less legally.

It was under threat. Everything I had sacrificed, my soul, was now plagued by an invisible menace. I toyed with the idea that it was the man in the pinstripe suit himself, but each time he came to the farm, he was charming, never a cross word, no sense of betrayal. He was happy, satisfied with the small favour I was doing for him. He liked my potatoes; they were great camouflage, it seems, in which to hide heroin and move it around mainland Europe. A small hole and the inside hollowed out slightly—just big enough to hold an ounce of pure heroin in its cradle—the spider in the nest is just as easily hidden.

The last time I saw him, he told me profits were up and gave me a percentage. I had changed nothing, held no extra for him in the barn, had no input, but he told me with a smile on his face that his associates had started to mix in additives, breaking down the purity but increasing the profit margin. Who cared if the customer noticed? Like the cow that ends up on the plate of the man who hasn't eaten meat for a month, they soon accept the impurity if they feel nourished.

I had drifted off, a week of no sleep finally catching up on me, paranoia exhausting me, wearing me out, dragging me under. I saw treachery everywhere. Who was watching me? The police? Interpol? The man in the suit? Or some other unnamed, unthought-of nosy intruder? Perhaps someone who wanted a cut of the money I had earned in order to save the farm…

I awoke with a start, a cry in the dark, a high-pitched squeal, fox-like, piercing the air of the outside world, light now. I heard a noise from the kitchen; who was up at this time of the day? It was followed by the sound of a pan dropping to the floor in panic as they also heard the scream of the fox in the coop.

My wife ran into the room where I was sitting, not bolt upright but cautious and alert. I'd got them; I'd got my spy. She looked at me, her face white, and I asked what she was doing up so early. I had, it seemed, slept beyond my usual time, and the day had chased the night far over the Spanish and African coastlines. Her panic transferred to me as easily as an inconsequential drop of blood in a syringe passed between two users of the white powder turned liquid.

She rushed out into the yard, and there was that scream again, and this time I knew for sure it wasn't a fox. I had caught the person trying to steal my home.

It came from a bush not thirty metres from the front door of the farm. I cocked my rifle and stalked the noise as it reached out to its saviour. I moved closer, keeping my wife behind me, urging her to stay back just in case the fellow, the fox, was also armed.

My sanity broke when I realised the scream was it calling for its mother and father. It was calling out in pain to my wife and me. My daughter—inquisitive, powerful imagination, a badger of black and white hair—had been caught in the trap I had carefully laid out for another, her arm soaked in blood that ran into the rusted metal gripping her tightly.

15.

The Young Knight's Tale 3: On The Ramblas

I HAVE ALWAYS ADORED Barcelona. It could have been a very different story, though; this part of my life could have seen me become a seedy and disreputable man. Perhaps I am that anyway. In my head, I have always believed myself to be a good man. Fallible, yes. I have lied to save my skin. I have told tall tales to improve my chances of getting on in life after failing miserably at the start. I have stolen to keep from starving, but I am a good man. Just circumstances sometimes arise where steps must be taken to survive or get ahead.

Barcelona holds mystic qualities for me. It is a city that makes sense—grid-shaped, ordered and unjumbled. It is historic, and it is not shy or coy in making its beauty known to the first-time visitor. Nor does it stray in its affections; it is a middle-aged lady, prim and proper, tidy, clean, no lousy eggs hatching underneath the brightly coloured skirts and often too readily applied make-up. Orwell said it best in *Homage to Catalonia*: 'I would sooner be a foreigner in Spain than in most countries. How easy it is to make friends in Spain!'

I had no friends in Spain, but there was trouble, a result of bad timing, of a trade that was making its way through Europe like the Black Death and feeding my own selfish need to stay alive.

Being a foreigner in Spain is a delight. I have walked The Ramblas since that day and been enchanted, played by and kissed whilst my inner pocket was fumbled with discreetly; being poor, on the run and desperate is quite another thing.

With help from my French teacher, I was given several hours head start before I was notified as missing—enough time to cover many miles, to get as far away as I could, to disappear into the crowd and hide in plain sight. Paris was beautiful; I regret not seeing more of that city. I have never been back since the kiss on the cheek from the woman who saved me from persecution, the whisper of good luck and a one-way ticket as far as Toulouse in my pocket. That is the memory of Paris I wish to preserve.

She was questioned, of course, but nothing stuck. She was a wonderful liar; I believed her to be an exceptional woman, a strong woman, one to admire fully for her brains and her attitude to life. I hope she knows that I never once forgot her.

The train journey was uneventful. I wish I could tell you a story or two, embellish the tale and make it sound even vaguely more exciting than it was. Dull does not compare, and to a young lad whose life had been turned upside down in the last year—actually all his life—this was perhaps the most serene, laid-back and utterly void of any type of mischief or harm journey undertaken. At one point, a sense of romanticism swept over me and I believed I should get off the train early, walk the rest of the way. I let my imagination flow, heroism and bravery the watchwords; it was an illusion I managed to maintain until the train came to a measured halt in Toulouse.

The crossing became more difficult from there, though still nothing spectacular: soaked by rain, feeling hungry and tired, but on the whole, pretty unremarkable. I remember reading about two young Irish boys who had told their parents they were going out and that they would not be late for dinner. Not only were they late for dinner that night, they ended up having breakfast at JFK airport, having managed to sneak aboard a Dart train, then a boat to Wales and finally getting on board a plane to America. At that point, as I kept out of sight of cars passing me, scared they were the type to keep an eye out for a runaway boy from England, and pleading with every lorry driver to give me a lift, I envied those two lads from Ireland. An adventure worth every mile, they crossed the ocean with their dreams.

Toulouse may be a very beautiful city, but she held no mystery. I wandered around, trying to hitch a ride to Barcelona. One person asked too many questions; one truck driver seemed far too eager to help, and I was repulsed by his glaring eyes and his lecherous leer. I didn't care if he was gay, but I didn't want to be fending someone off most of the way, only for that person to then dob me in if he was pulled over—to suggest I was a bigger quarry than he was for breaking a local speed limit.

Finally, I found someone. I was in luck all the way to Barcelona—what I thought to be my final destination. I could lie low there, get a job waiting tables, anything. I had escaped home and would not go back. Luck runs for only a short while; if you are truly fortunate and able to keep the accident of chance interested in you then you can, perhaps, conquer mountains and become a champion; keep her wrapped in furs and laden with diamonds and you can become a king.

Luck for the ordinary, those who misuse her, who make a bargain with her—'get me this and I won't ask anything more'… until they do—take advantage of her good nature. The small bet accumulator turns into a permanent fixture down at the bookmaker's until eventually the double ones start rolling and you owe a few months' pay packets to the snake eyes behind the Plexiglas screen and their *don't care it is my job to enforce this rule* voices.

I'd had my share of double sixes; I'd rolled them consecutively, kissed the dots on that side of the face, flirted with luck to the point of only stopping short of a fumble after dark and picking the straw from her hair as she smiled. Now, she turned nasty and snarled like an abandoned lover, demanding she keep all I had lavished upon her before tossing me aside for a better-looking model, one fit to be seen on her arm.

Luck discarded me the evening of my first day in Barcelona. I was presentable but looked young—a couple of café owners openly laughed and asked where my parents were. One threw his shoe at me and then, with an edge of trepidation, I noticed an English newspaper had been left to rot on a lattice table, folded up but with its cover on the inside. The owner had long since gone off into the night in search of enlightenment or a place in which to find luck lurking, her own flirtation, her need always ready.

Turning the paper over to read from front to back, I was taken aback to find my picture on the front cover with the title parading in black, rigid, regimented, square-back-and-shoulders tight type:

MISSING BOY: ABSCONDED FROM SCHOOL TRIP

Thankfully, the picture they had used was one that was a year or two out of date. I had not been in a paper since I was a baby with a hypodermic needle hanging out of my arm, a scar reminding me of my mother's stupidity and need to dwell on the loss of innocence. How much did they know about me? I felt ill with the answer brewing inside my mind.

I had learned to distrust journalists from an early age. One of my so-called guardians had dropped some hints when I was around the age of six to a friend of a friend, the local damage juice masquerading as beer opening up his mouth just a little too wide, a little too friendly.

She kept spiders, you know. She watched her own mother kill her father, who knows what over. Who knows the damage it did to her—no wonder she started using drugs… Ah, poor little bastard that he is, she tried to kill him, you know.

It wasn't word for word, but the insinuation was there. They also managed to add carefully, as an undercurrent, the undermining thread, that the previous year had seen me questioned in relation to the mysterious death of the school's headmaster. An overwhelming tiredness consumed me. No rage, anger or desperation, I was not going to get caught, not here—it was still too close to home—but at that moment, any fight I had was wiped out as easily as a bleach-soaked cloth swiped over a table where raw meat had been prepared.

The memory of being bombarded with questions, being expected to have opinions at such a young age, to understand the world and your place in it, the connections and the pain that existed before you were even born—nobody can answer those prying enquiries. I was moved on again to another foster family within a day or two of that potential bomb of a story exploding. I had been saved from appearing in that paper by the good work of the social services. The journalist had been threatened, his editor likewise.

Resolved in my efforts but suffering from quite severe pangs of hunger, I walked away from the table, careful to rip the front page off and throw it in the nearest bin—if only all journalism could be treated so.

I made a mental note of how much money I had in my pocket: enough for a couple of days of walking around during the day and pretending I was a tourist—ironically, I could just say I was on a school trip if I was asked—but not enough to find somewhere to sleep. However, food was the most overriding issue. I paced the shops and outdoor cafés, places that would not give a reasonably polite English boy a job but would take his last penny for a bottle of lemonade or a bite of the local cuisine.

Desperation was not in my nature but neither was going hungry, and for the first time since I had come up with the plan to run away, I felt the desire to undo it. I had been reckless, stupid, irresponsible to my own well-being, but then I also felt elation. For the first time in my life, I realised I was wanted, not in the same way that girls might want to be seen with you, but as the geeky rebel with a story to tell, someone to show to their dad to get a reaction from him, the careful word in your ear to not mess with his daughter while the mother smiles brightly and offers you more tea, internally sobbing at the fact their daughter would now be the one to dictate the terms of their relationship.

I was wanted. I was a man on the loose, not dangerous or likely to cause you harm but a troubled individual who was needed back home. Well, home, for all that it was worth, could screw itself.

I plucked up the courage and grabbed a couple of apples from a local vendor, one swiftly making its way into my coat pocket. I gave him the exact money for its now solitary mate and smiled. A big, bearded grin bade me thank you and turned quickly away to greet its next willing customer.

I wandered on down The Ramblas, colours and exotic shouting, instantly turned-out drawings for the excitable tourists relieved of their pesetas and, if not careful, eased of their purses and their wallets at the same time. Birds for sale, caged and looking decidedly unhealthy but whom a small child could befriend before the bird dropped down dead on the floor of its cage a couple of weeks later. I took it all in, the juice of the apple running down my throat, the sideshow of The Ramblas, the smells, the danger, the glory and the abundance of light. Yet look deeper: for every firework in the sky, there is a patch of dark that surrounds it.

With all plans comes a fall. Mine was to believe I could just blend in, become at home in a foreign city and go on as I had before, somehow pull myself up and become a big man. What utter nonsense we install into our childish minds. What was the point of that? Did I think I was eventually going home, back to the town from which I had absconded? Was I going back covered in glory? *I found my way in life, and this is how I did it, come revel with me, buy me a beer and I will reveal all.* That is just showing off, the product of a mind that wants to punish those around it who made it feel incomplete, lonely and abused.

A plan; no throwing the dice. This was not about luck. I needed to get out of Barcelona, out of Spain, and have no trace of who I once was. A new name, a new beginning, snake eyes surrounding me. Easy: stow away on a boat, crawl into the middle of the sea, find someone who didn't speak English or didn't even care and enquire who I was, a fisherman, a trawler, a passage boat, perhaps get to one of the islands.

My mind raced with possibilities, and as I thought, I made my way down to the harbour. I had to see for myself just what types of vessels there were, if they were easy to hide in or if I could openly suggest how much of a benefit I could be to the captain.

Romanticism never dies, it just changes shape. It adds texture to your thoughts and makes your dreams ever more feel like dying a slow dreadful death. I was no poet back then; I had only the slightly tarnished soul of a teenage boy who liked to talk to girls and who used lyrics and poetry to appear deep and moody. It was romanticism that made me look at the boats with a keen eye and wonder how impossible this next step might be.

I think I got too close to one of the boats and may have stumbled upon a group of fishermen who didn't take kindly to being scrutinised by young eyes. In fact, I didn't even see the men until a couple of them came over and started talking abruptly and with menace, pointing at me, swearing, fingers poking me in the chest, and then, when I tried to reason with them, tried to explain all I was doing was looking at their boats, that I found their work inspirational, that *Moby Dick* was a profound novel and they should be proud of their heritage, one of them punched me so hard in the face the bruise came up almost immediately.

I staggered backwards. Such was the violence meted out to me, any cockiness, any self-assurance I may have built up in the last couple of hours was blown out of the water. He punched me again, and the message was clear: fuck off, keep away.

I sat back down in The Ramblas, a glass of water going warm and a cup of tea coming from the opposite direction. I had a cloth on my face; blood had congealed and padded on my chin. My nose had taken the brunt of the swelling; the ache had me worried for a while. I thought it was broken.

No adventure, just a quiet life, one in which to start again. Barcelona in less than a day had been a steep learning curve. It had pushed me, prodded me, made me nervous and finally punched me in the face. I admit that I came close to getting up out of the seat, finding a policeman and asking to go home. *Sorry, sir, I will be a good boy. I will keep my thoughts to myself, and you can reward me by continually probing about my mother.*

I don't give up that easily. I may panic, I might shudder in the face of a fist coming out of nowhere, but I have, or at least used to possess, pride and stubbornness. I was getting out of Barcelona. I was going to go home, and a boat from the harbour was the only way. I was not to know right at that moment that it would take me nearly three weeks to achieve, that I was not going where I'd planned, and that the bind to my mother would be rigid tight.

I am very nearly at the end, my friend. This tale is almost over, you see. There is probably so much I have left out, that I have forgotten to impart, but then, you just want details. You are just like that journalist, are you not? Searching for answers that do not exist, confirmations to the suspicions that rattle around inside your head like a marble in a can.

Barcelona—I liked that city, but I would never go back there as a sixteen-year-old boy. I would never go back there without a penny in my pocket, because she is cruel when you are down. Luck and the pulse of a city—there are only so many times you can throw snake eyes before a double six comes back around again.

16.

When Death Calls: A Tale of Finality

IN FRONT OF me, caught in the glare of the headlights of my driver's car, was the body of one of the policemen I had placed on guard duty outside the doctor's house. The small drive that led to the iron, red-painted gates gave no indication of what we might find, and as far as I was concerned, the destruction was going to be found inside. My friend's life was not only in danger but it was falling apart around him. The seams were all fraying, coming loose, and soon, he would have nothing left.

I was surprised we had not been met by nosy neighbours, ready to offer explanations for the gunshots that had disturbed their sleep, their lovely evening meal...the sense of dread they felt that something had gone terribly wrong...that they were ready to talk to the local paper, to the television...that they would make a bit of cash off the back of the man they always thought was peculiar but who—with the strain of a tear forming at the corner of their eye and a sincere look to the camera—they would laud as a model citizen, a pretty stand-up guy.

That last bit went through my mind as I leaned over the body of the dead constable. 'It all boils down to money', a detective once wrote. I forget who now, but he was spot on. Those who kill soon exploit and open up a market that is the envy of free enterprise.

Yet there had been no one. The last couple of hundred metres or so had been in total darkness, not a flicker of light to be seen. No candles, no flashlights, no wasting of electricity from a television through a thin veiled curtain. It were almost as if they had been warned to not be around, in the same way that the so-called boat owners had been given advance warning. Something was rotten on this island, something in a suit and with a large enough reach to make sure his bidding was done: silent, effective and dangerous.

The blood from the constable's head no longer flowed. It had been some time since the man was shot, execution style, in the back of the head, his brain matter strewn across several feet, and I noted that the forensic team—a handful of people, run by a man with an iron grip and little humour—would be rubbing their hands in glee at the thought of overtime. I went back to the car and told the driver what I had seen, that he was to report it immediately—as soon as he was away from the gates, at least half a mile. I had already lost one officer tonight; I wasn't prepared to lose another.

I walked to the gates and opened them a notch further than they had been left. I presumed the other constable had been instructed to go inside with Dutch, to act as a backup in case of tension. For him, it might have been the lesser of two evils to happen in the last twenty minutes.

All the lights were blazing around the property itself, and whilst I could not see the doctor's study, the one room that led directly out to his garden and then towards the cliffs and the sheer drop to the rocks and the sea below, I suspected that in there, the lights were ablaze. The question remained if there was anyone home.

Despite the crunch of the gravel path beneath my feet, I kept more than ear out for the sound of the unexpected hiding in the bushes that I might have missed when shining my torch into the abyss, something surprising not lit up by the carnival ride of the house, the absolute circus the last week had become. I arrived at the door and again found it was slightly ajar, the inside light bathing me, sending me temporarily blind and as if I had been enveloped by some torture device used to extract information. I felt as if I were being probed, pushed for an answer to which I had only just started to unravel the question.

I heard Dutch's voice call out to me, and she fumbled on the wall to turn off the light, shouting instructions to the other constable I had left on guard to go around the house and turn off every light that was on. In hindsight, I should have countermanded her order and told her to keep them on. They, whoever they might be, would be able to see us but we would surely also be able to see them.

Being temporarily blinded is a weird sensation to those who regularly see. The world is out of kilter; you become suddenly aware of your fragility, of being exposed and vulnerable. Then, as each second passes, your sight is restored, and for a while you want to go up to anybody without sight and shake their hand, tell them how much you admire their bravery and fortitude. Like everything else in life, the feeling soon fades, and you find yourself forgetting, the empathy lost until the next time someone turns on the light and shines it directly into your eyes.

In the now darkness of the reception area, I saw Dutch's outline, and she begged me follow to her into the study. What greeted me there was illuminated chaos, a carnival of clowns that had ransacked the big top, opened the lion's cage and allowed it to run riot, shit everywhere and back the tamer into a corner. I hated circuses; I disliked the falseness of it all and only had sheer disgust for the way they operated. Yet here, in a study in which I had sat many times, sampling good whisky and the comfort of friendship, I saw what the circus could do to those immersed in it.

Everywhere on the floor were thousands of pounds, a carpet of money, strewn to the wind, some crumpled, littering the room like ticker-tape after a hero has been made welcome down an American street, and, according to Dutch, each one as worthless as that same ticker-tape in the morning-after clean-up.

I bent down and picked one up, staring at my friend who sat, defeated and exhausted, on the floor, his hands behind his back in a position of meekness and hell. I enquired if he was under arrest, if Dutch or the fellow officer wanted to pursue the shot fired or the fact he had threatened them with violence and a pistol. Obviously some talking had been going on whilst I had been on my way to the house, and they had agreed it was nothing, a heat-of-the-moment exchange; no damage had been done. I saw her eyes flash to the constable and then to the books on the wall and noticed that at least one thing tonight had perished at the hands of a man driven mad.

I ordered the constable to unlock the handcuffs and get my friend to his chair. I brushed a few of the counterfeit notes off the leather seat and watched as he was gently seated, no fight, no reckless abandon, no war left in him. Dutch broke the small silence and told me that the money was not all; she handed me the deed of sale of the yacht, and I saw he had been completely done over. In his greed, he had overlooked the wording of the contract.

He had been screwed all ways, and how. I am no lawyer, but it basically amounted to this: he still owned the vessel sitting at the bottom of the harbour. Greed, and a momentarily fling with a woman who was part of the trap to bring him down. He had sold the boat in good faith, and now he was paying the price for wanting to get off the island in a hurry.

No wonder he looked so defeated by life. All this time, he had been a rock. He had escaped hardship and persecution in England, he had been my friend when I didn't deserve it, and he had built up a hell of a reputation in the academic world. OK, so he had slept with my ex-wife, but in his favour he'd also made sure I would never take her back. Was that the point of that tryst? He was saving me from ever having to deal with her again, knowing I would not sleep with a woman he had taken for himself?

I don't know why, but I thought of our son at that moment. Long dead, cold and scattered to the wind, a series of childhood diseases had taken him, and the final one, measles, had left him weak, almost unable to function, his eyes unblinking, unfocused and haunted, his fight all lost. It was the same look on the face of my friend, a man who had so little left to fight for.

He spoke briefly, just a few words, but they conveyed everything I had thought.

"I am finished."

The dismay of the police phone cackling snapped my attention to the matter at hand. My driver had managed to get in touch with headquarters and had also found a place to park the car out of sight. I congratulated him and told him to wait there until backup arrived. He responded in the worst way, telling me he had noticed a car with blacked-out number plates come down the road, and he'd followed them on foot until he saw them push the gates open wide and drive in, almost running over the fallen officer.

I turned off the phone and looked into Dutch's eyes. So little time for explanations, no precious moments to take the dead man's fellow officer aside and tell him his partner on the beat had been shot by those who were now coming for us.

I had to think fast. I scooped up a couple of counterfeit notes, ordered Dutch to open the patio doors out onto the garden and tell the policeman that, despite everything, if he wanted to see justice done tonight, then to help me get the doctor out of the house as quickly as possible.

I sensed what was going to happen. I could see the same operation being employed a second time. They were going to burn everything to the ground, and if we were not careful, this time we would also go up in flames.

The first explosion came a little after a minute later. My friend was unwilling to leave the cocoon of his chair, his mind focusing on all he had lost, all he seemingly cared for. I shouted down his ear at the same time as a small grenade came rattling through the grand entrance, all marble and wood, soon to be all dust and scorch.

I had no intention of going out this way. I knew the garden offered not salvation, but if we could get close to the cliff edge, at least we'd have a choice to go down fighting or jump into the raging sea and hope help came before we were swept away and the investigation with us. I had no issue with fire, I had witnessed and felt its pull many times over the years. I wouldn't say I was drawn to it, but I was certainly enamoured enough to watch it consume to the final ember, until the final flight of a lonely cinder dropped to the ground and died screaming like Icarus.

My friend stumbled, and in that motion, I went down on one knee. I urged both the constable and Dutch to run, to get to the bottom of the garden and lie low. I saw in her face the unwillingness to leave me behind; I had no idea until that point that she truly regarded me with something other than professional courtesy. What did she see in me? Perhaps it was not for me to know.

A smaller explosion reverberated around the room. I figured that was the living room under attack. I grabbed my friend by the arm once more and pulled him without ceremony upwards and onwards to the patio door. I heard shouting, a warning followed by a hail of bullets and then a creak as a few damaged timber beams fell and crashed in the hallway. It bought us time.

I have no idea how it happened, but my friend came alive in that moment, as I prepared myself for another shock wave or fireball to come down upon our heads, the punishment from above for our collected sins, whatever they may have been. He shouted and pushed me on, causing me to slip once again and this time bring the full weight of my body down upon my knee. He staggered back towards his desk and pulled out papers, letting them mingle in the aftermath of his false hero parade and the thousands of counterfeit notes. I watched, perplexed, and ducked as one final round of gun fire came close by and small splinters blew across the air.

He had what he was searching for in his hand and shakily hurried back to me. It was sublime, that moment. It was stupid and daft and so very like him. He grabbed my arm and pulled me up just as a gunman burst into the room, his left arm on fire, but judging by his face, he truly did not care. This was a man paid to do one job, and he was going to make sure it was done.

My friend was in the firing line, and my gun was in between us. I could not get my hands to it to get off a shot in retaliation. If the gunman's aim was true, he could take us both down before we even had a chance to say goodbye.

His aim was only slightly off as his arm shook with the heat of the flames. One bullet fired, straight into the side of my friend's stomach, before the crack of a wooden frame came down upon his head.

The doctor slumped forward, but such was his momentum we were able to get through the patio doors and out into the garden. Before us was the figure of the young detective from the Netherlands, and with a swoop, she picked up the injured man and ran back to the relative safety of the nearby cliff edge.

I looked behind me. The whole house was ablaze. All that work, all that effort, and for what? I knew this was to be the final humiliation for my friend. His trial would be over, found guilty by a man who had allowed his anger to fester, to grow and become even more evil than I had bargained for.

Through the sound of a life becoming meaningless, I heard my radio go, my driver shouting out for all he was worth that help was on the way, and that he had just seen the unlicensed car drive away at top speed but he was sure there had been only two people in the vehicle and not the three he had first seen and followed. He told me to be careful; one was obviously still there pursuing me and the others. I told him to not worry; the third man was down, and if he was still alive, he wouldn't be for long.

I told my driver to make sure those who were coming—the fire brigade, paramedics and ambulance drivers—were careful of our fallen comrade. They needed to do the decent thing by him first. We were all right, battered and bruised, and the house was only fit for a smouldering ruin. I didn't have the heart to tell him the doctor had been hit; I figured it was only a flesh wound, a couple of weeks in hospital, a bullet hole to add to the stories with which he could beguile his future students. Knowing him, there would be a book of poetry to accompany him restarting his life.

I walked to the end of the garden and watched my colleagues get up and dust themselves down. My friend stayed on the ground but smiled when he saw my soot-covered face and wincing manner as my knee protested under the exertion of the night. He signalled to me to bend down, and as I did so, he handed to me a couple of files and a ring binder, his final offering to the world.

All he had left was in that gesture. There would be no more books, no tours, no sex on a yacht again. With a slight moan and what sounded like an apology, he took his last fleeting breath and died.

This was the night poetry grappled with Death and the figure in black finally won.

17.

A Tale of Madness Under Observation

A NEW PROCEDURE, SOMETHING to wake the mind up. That's what he said to me as we sat watching, through the one-way mirror, his psychiatrist talk to her.

She had been under my care for a couple of years; they all had. I guess, once this gets out, once they notify the authorities of the failings in our security protocols, I shall be facing a disciplinary and removal from this establishment. I won't say it's not fair. I screwed up. I have, it seems, been part of a deceit that has caused a patient of mine to die, to take her own life, violently and without aid, at least, not from my own staff.

He first contacted me about six months ago with a simple letter of introduction, a well-presented résumé and an implied curiosity I could not fail to notice in a man of learning. On any other day, I may have put the letter aside and asked my secretary to add it to the daily round-up of papers to be shredded and burnt, but there was something about the way he wrote with knowledge of the mind, how he was involved in new ways of thinking. It made me stay the execution by shredder and keep it on file for a month or two.

Was it my vanity it appealed to? I have seen hundreds of requests and demands to interview those under my care, from psychiatry students wishing to submit a paper on X to those wishing to follow up on a story for a potential book or journalistic piece on Y. Each and every one I turned down, I told them no.

Vanity is a horrible thing. To some degree, Detective, we all suffer from it. Whether it is in the hope of a compliment on how we look, how we are perceived, the way we dress, our ability, wealth or happiness, those little flourishes of words get under our skin and provide us with a small sense of gratification. Stroke anyone's ego hard enough and eventually they will come round to your way of thinking.

A couple of months went past, and to be honest, I had barely given the man a thought. Routine is as important for the staff as it is for those under our care; the same faces, if possible, at all times; no sudden noises or moves which could be considered a threat; keep the peace; don't let their delusions, their fears and their past get in the way of progress. Just keep it calm, one step at a time, and all is good for the facility.

I came here from London two years ago, a promotion of sorts, although when it comes to mental health, the private sector does not have that kind of hierarchy. You just become good at your job, leave the NHS and let those poor buggers get used to the next person in charge. It's like running the country; you get used to one group of inmates and nurses, and then it's all change. A new idiot is put in power and the whole edifice crumbles and has to get patched up again.

This facility is not like that. In here, stable means exactly that. In here, strong is not just a buzz word for a politician to bandy around and turn into a mantra for how the country will fall at the feet of their newly installed messiah and all will be well. In here, I feel sympathy for those institutionalised by years of their own madness. Out there on the streets, where they divide and fall over the pettiest of arguments on their mobile devices, heads down, always tapping out the same beliefs and false thoughts…well, I sometimes wonder exactly who really is mad, who are the ones in a room surrounded by their own bubble and echoing thoughts.

Two months ago, I receive a phone call. It was him, the man with the confident and alluring proposition. He gave me several more references but was insistent that I talk to a professor he had recently worked with in Paris, conducting tests on patients. He told me the results were startling and gave me a number. Intrigued, I rang the professor immediately.

Vanity—it has been humanity's curse for as long as there has been someone with an ego to kiss, a passage to flatter or something of value the other person covets. In my case, it seems two out of three really is bad.

I spoke with the professor for what seemed an absolute age, and by the time I finally put the phone down, it was agreed that both men would come to the facility the following Monday morning and take a look at one of our more interesting cases. What possessed me? What came over me to allow two unknown men to come and witness our work here, to upset the balance of the facility before this all goes too far, before the chance to retract anything comes along? The way to flatter me, it seems, is to offer money to improve the complex. It also helped that over the previous couple of months, my own personal fiscal arrangements had gone sour.

I don't even know how it happened. I have thought about it since, but nothing pointed me in the direction of how money just seemed to be going out of my account. The first indication was when my wife rang to say she had gone into town to purchase a present for a friend's wedding anniversary. Nothing sinister in that; it was money from a joint account we used for such things, and there should have been enough money in there to pay for those small incidentals—the off-the-cuff ticket for a night at the theatre, the small keepsake from a rare day out or even just to pay for a takeaway when neither of us can be bothered to cook.

It is a slush fund owned by two people who normally cover their backsides when it comes to money.

Money—it is the root of all desire. Have enough and all of a sudden it changes you, turns your own worth against you. I have never wanted to be poor, but, of course, I never intended to be rich either. A conflict of interests, my upbringing doing battle against the consumerist world we have come to milk like a cow in a pen, several teats all at once dispensing cash, whilst the poor old farmer suddenly finds he is worse off than when his grandfather used to hire a milkmaid. Our small slush fund went one afternoon, a present not purchased; I rang the bank that evening.

All seemed resolved. An accounting error, they said, money replaced the next day, a letter of apology would be making its way to us. Sure enough, the following morning, my wife went to the shops and came home with a small gift for our friends and a new tie for me to wear in the evening.

That cow often gets over-milked; the machine is not empathetic when it comes to the distress calls of a solitary beast. As long as the line keeps going, as long as someone down the line is making cheese, then what does it matter?

The following Monday, I invited the two guests in and was immediately struck by their manners and their knowledge of some of the cases we had in the facility. All above the level, my employers had obviously given them some background on the patients. They had done their research. We talked professionally, and almost light-heartedly, a working plan came together. Over the next four weeks, the professor would work closely with one of the people under our care and then submit both his findings and any improvements noted to both me and my employers.

I had just the person in mind: a young man who had been abused by his wife, beaten, submitted to torture, brought to the very lows of depression and then taken further. It was a wonder he was alive, really. Her final act before she had been caught was to start putting poison in his food, a small addition of narcotic in every meal. To the outside world, she presented herself as the very model of sincerity; in the marital home. she was ruthless and deranged. I would have loved to have had her in my facility. It would have been interesting to see how such a mind worked, the untouched potential and devastation in someone on their way to becoming a murderer.

They wanted to discuss it further. Yes, the man had merit, but his was an abuse that was fresh. He had been here under our care for only six months, and he was already showing improvement. He was, in their words, a statistic. He was doing well, of that there was no doubt, but it was an under-researched area.

The manipulation by some women of their partners should not be ignored. Whilst not as prevalent as domestic abuse inflicted by men, it still seems an aberration of nature that could and should be investigated. I argued this case most strongly and continued after the professor's companion excused himself to use the bathroom.

The discussion between us whilst he was out of the room was friendly, but I could feel the man reaching with his opinion. His gaze was intense, purposeful and leading, but never once did I question his sincerity. His credentials looked very much in order, and the way he held himself, the way he talked, he could be nothing but of the very highest of standards. I felt fortunate, lucky, even, that they had come here.

The telephone rang; it was my secretary informing me that the bank were on hold, a small mix-up with a cheque, a payment for a broken window caused, we assumed, by teenagers playing football near the house. We didn't find out, but both my wife and I had our suspicions. I told my secretary I would come along now, to the outer office, and take it there. As I made my own excuses to the professor, his companion walked back in, slightly flustered by the apparent lack of towels in the bathroom, his hands damp and face sweating. I told him to wait a moment and I would get someone to fetch him a towel, and if they liked, they could have a small tour of the facility whilst I dealt with a minor issue.

The phone call was one that caused deep anxiety, confusion and anger. Not only had the cheque bounced but it had jumped so high that everything else in the account was now gone. I don't have a lot of money, Detective. This facility may be privately funded but it doesn't pay as well as you would believe. But I guess your own line of work is the same. Wherever you go, no matter what you do, you could always use a little more to ease yourself through to the next quarter, the following year.

I rang my wife. Thankfully, I had been the one to get the call and not her. She would have panicked; there would have been accusations; there would have been threats and a showdown, an ultimatum. You see, a few years ago I had a brief but tender affair. I fell quite hard for the person and considered the possibility of leaving my wife. It was my first and only such meeting—one that could have cost me my marriage and also cost me money. Not only did the person steal from me, when I tried to end it, they also tried to blackmail me for extra money.

My wife surprised me; she dealt with the situation calmly and efficiently. She saw to it that some of the money was recovered, and she managed to get the police involved without too much of a stain on my character. Talk always happens, though. Talk followed me in the job that I had before, and that's why I ended up here; a promotion, a sense of security, but one that came with a warning that if ever it happened again, she would be more aggressive with her words and actions.

The blackmailer was caught, I survived, they went to prison, I lost my wife's respect. Sometimes I think it would be better if I had taken my own life, such is the shame. It is shame I feel now, as I recall what happened when I told my wife to stay at her mother's until I picked her up. I was in a panic. Worse even than my wife would have been. I was always the weaker. She just pretended to defer to me so that my fragile ego would not think back to the day when I had to tell her of my embarrassing failure as a man and a husband.

I know now I had been played for a fool. A decent man in all but name, the cheapest of traps, their plan had worked. Such was the severity of the issue, I could not help but become agitated and distressed when I caught up with the two visitors. They somehow managed to manipulate the situation to their advantage. The companion took me aside and told me he could arrange for the professor to help me out. I started to wave the idea off.

"My problem," I said. "I will resolve it." He started to talk quickly, but still with exceptional manners. He told me he was sure it was just an issue at the bank, that all could be resolved, but why take the chance? Why see a problem arise? He would not take no for an answer. All he wanted in return was access to the woman, three or four sessions, the perfect case study, the makings of a book. I would get mentions, perhaps be back at the pinnacle of my profession.

Flattery, you see, opening up my own vanity case. I agreed but asked that it be considered a loan only; as my bank realised the problem, I would be able to level with them.

It was the hand on the shoulder that caught me off guard, his gentle manner now persuasive. He was in control and I had lost the fight. He asked me for my bank's number and spoke to the manager when he got through. Quickly, efficiently, he quoted my account number, which I had written down for him, and then walked down the corridor; leaving me alone with my nerves and the professor for human company.

I believe in sex they call it double-teamed. I had been played from the front and the back, and I hadn't even noticed my trousers coming loose and my shirt being tucked up. The professor raised his eyebrows and smiled diligently, as if being caught in the same position. He continued to smile as he said, with an obvious glee in his tone, "I would like to see the patient now."

I took him to her room and allowed him to look inside through the small window. He gestured to me to let him in. I was in no position to refuse; down the end of the corridor, I heard his companion's footsteps coming back with a brisk stride. Letting the professor in and then closing the door, I turned my attention back to the companion.

Being double-teamed by professionals is a real eye-opener. I realise now that I had been played for weeks. The broken window, the small matter of the slush fund, the bank account—they were behind it all, and now, in my confession to you, I understand that I am not getting out of this one.

One last chance, she said. Don't screw up our lives again, she insisted.

What have I done? The patient is dead because of me. I allowed the professor to get inside her head, to see the damage done to her. She responded, became alert for a week or two, then suddenly she was dead—smashed her own brains out on a wall.

Every man has his weakness, his vanity. Mine was suddenly finding I had fifty thousand pounds in my account, a reward for my efforts, an advance on sales of the book for which I would be heavily praised and quoted. Vanity, sheer vandalism of the soul. My soul, her death.

I was once a good man, you know. A good husband, a willing participant in the community, a friend to all. Now what? What do I do now, when it becomes public that you have spoken to me, when it gets back to my wife and she makes me talk? I will have nothing; a weak man with no pity or life.

I heard her speak, just the once, through the flap in the door. She was sorry for all the problems she had caused her son. She genuinely wept when she was told what she had done to him. I believe she was told he had died. I wasn't aware of that—such a waste of a life, drowning at sea.

18.

A Tale of Broken Thoughts: Her Final Moments

IS THAT TAPE recorder working? Is that camera above your head the one you will study for telltale signs and tics, obvious symptoms and spasms from which you can say with scientific accuracy that this was the moment of breakthrough, that you can declare with certainty that I am mad?

Let me tell you now: I am gone. I am wasted, and after today, I will not speak again. My story is over, and why? Because I have lost faith in it all. I will tell you all I want you to know and then that is it; you can all join me in hell.

Hell. For years, I've dismissed the notion. It is just here, the seventh circle. Dante was mistaken. Hell is being force-fed, being told that you can be rehabilitated, the mix of wanting to be my friend and then convincing me I am undeserving of such sympathy. The handshake from someone who hates you with a passion, the look of disgrace and humiliation, the desire to cause you harm from the person who professes you friend. Hell… I have seen and lived in hell.

I had spiders when I was little. Exotic for after the war, and not the thing for a young girl to have in her room, but they fascinated me—their mating habits, the way they devoured the one they allowed to have sex with them, their prowess, their durability, the way they capture prey, the way they can die with a simple stamp. The other children in the village shied away from me, they said I was nuts, completely off my trolley, and perhaps they had a point. I was the product of an unstable relationship, a man who fell into my mother's life and was dispatched in the same casual manner: brutal, quick and without mercy.

Spiders are majestic, are they not? They are regal, almost pure. People are fallible. They regard life as something far too complex. They keep searching for a hidden meaning, for domain, for the extra thrill—surely the prospect of the hunt should be enough, and yet, when it boiled down to it, when it came to that final test, I also failed. I became hedonistic. The thrill of the hunt was gone and all I wanted was to sink into oblivion, to not be anywhere near another human being again.

Is my son still alive? They won't tell me. They won't tell me if I killed him—I didn't mean to if I did. I didn't mean to put that syringe into his body. I just wanted us to go to sleep together, to escape the madness of conformity and order I once craved and instead revel in the dreams, the freedom and the nightmares.

Nightmares are important; they keep your pulse racing. Anybody can dream—anybody can see a different realm with endless possibilities and feel the glory of the multicoloured effects—but the nightmares, the black-and-white and grainy… Fear drives us to a purpose; nightmares project an objective to survive. I don't want to live anymore, I have killed my child, and now I just want to fade away, sink into my own dreams.

It took a while to make sense of my mother's drastic attack on my father—his murder. Why she just suddenly assailed him, why the knife was so quick at its job, took time for me to understand…

He died, but not at my hands. He died on a boat outside of Barcelona…

Spiders. I have been fascinated by them all my life. Some girls squeal the first time they see them, that childhood primordial state of something crawling, poking out from behind the poster on the wall, the black spot in the bath or the sink that is all fur and moves like a disease across Europe during the time of the plague. Boys are terrified of them, perhaps a yearning in them to emulate the fire in their hearts, the potential arsonists in the making, as they watch them scoot up the wall like flickering flames. Put two or three of them together and they act like a firestorm, a raging spectacle of triggered discharge, the fever of several sparks of bonfire sizzling on the ground before being stamped out in fear; the fear of being burnt, the fright of being bitten.

I first held a spider when I was a little girl. My mother almost slapped it out of my hand, urging me to drop it, that it was filthy, that it was horrid and that nice girls didn't do such things. A spider is an elegant, focused, pure and dividing creature. Almost everybody loves a dog, the dopey eyes, the slobber, the bundling over in the mud and rain when walking them—a dog is just fun with a stick in its mouth and fleas in its coat. Cats…you have to be some sort of fiend to like cats. Obstinate, possessive, aloof and spiteful, I cannot abide them. They treat you like dirt and then expect you to feed them—sounds like an abuse relationship to me.

Did he die by drowning or did he burn and choke on the fumes as the boat caught fire? You have to answer me, please, tell me.

I heard shouting coming from downstairs—nothing new really, nothing that hadn't happened a hundred times over the last couple of years. Nothing that mean more than being told to stay in my room all night, to block my ears and pray for the morning. Nothing always begets nothing. The morning would come, and either they would act as if nothing had happened, or one of the two would be gone for a few days, the only trace their lingering sharp tongue and the evidence of bruising on the other.

More times than not, it was my mother's hand upon my father's face. He bore a scar just above his right eye which he said was a war wound that he'd stopped covering up. He often had bruises on his arms, and once I noticed a couple of cigarette burns in his left palm. Apparently, he didn't listen the first time. Not that he wasn't averse to hitting back. A couple of times, I saw my mum nursing a black eye, and once her arm was in a sling after he twisted it too far. The funny thing is I never once saw these displays of male aggression. I did see, however, the acts of violence created by my mother.

Shouting. I hate shouting, hate arguments, hate the way they fester and explode out of control. I hate the way they escalate like a war, tit for tat. Prolonged or short-lived, I hated the Vietnam War, or was it the Korean War? They are all the same in the end.

There was a knife sticking out of his chest. "Oh my god!" she shouted. "Call for an ambulance."

I was a good wife until I was introduced to heroin. An addictive personality should not be introduced to such evil things, and yet it was nice. All the way through pregnancy, I managed to stay off it. I was clean and sober throughout; any hang-ups were in the past. My father was dead, my mother had wasted away in jail, spared the death penalty by a few months, Ruth Ellis having the dubious honour of being the last woman to hang. Personally, I would have let my mother dangle in her place. There is murder and then there is manipulative evil.

All lies… Lies. You are a liar, a liar, a goddamn dirty liar. Get out of my room, get out, get out, get out.

***

I'm sorry. I'm so tired, I didn't mean what I said yesterday. I didn't want you to get out. I didn't mean to call you a liar. I just felt…oh, I don't know. I just felt you were going into my head too much. I am tired. I want to go back to my garden—can I please go back to my garden? Get out, go on. Get the fuck out of here. Stop injecting me with that stuff! You're making me remember things I don't want to…

***

Where have you been? You haven't been here for days—look, I counted, there on the wall. I marked down all the times that near-necrophilia-loving pervert came into the room—the nurse, the one who touches me up, who slides her hand up and down my leg when she's trying to get me eat. I noticed when she does that, the flowers in my garden sag, and it takes ages to perk them back up again. I waited for you…I never told you to go, did I? I never said that, surely. I would not do that. Thank you for giving me another shot. It helps, it really does…

I worry I cannot find my way back to my garden as well as I used to. It seems barren, and the surroundings are odd. I see a railway line in the distance where there was never one before, and each time I look up, there is the sign of new houses being built, invisible workmen tearing apart my view, open spaces and meadows filled with butterflies and the songs of sparrows consuming the air, now replaced by drains being put in the ground. What lives in drains? Bugs, nasty horrible bugs, the shit of humanity, blocked and never truly clean, viruses, bacteria—play around in the drain long enough and you end up becoming a leprous beast, a bug with the face of a clown.

Have you taken it away from me? Have you removed my view? Are you the one behind all those buildings going up and blocking the sunlight? If it was just one house, a nice garden of their own, not straight in front of me but somewhere out of my main sight, I wouldn't complain so much. But that view was always mine. What will I see eventually? An estate full of children, all noisy creatures, all exploring the drains and slowly eroding the meadow. Those bugs will spread. My spiders will not be able to eat them all, and they will be overwhelmed. They will become engulfed in the rising smell.

I looked out the other day, and there is now a tunnel underneath the railway line. It looks dead, no lights, I cannot see through it. If I squint really hard, it looks like there is a brick wall, that it's one-way only, closed off. What stupidity is that? What purpose does that bring? If I was to leave the safety of this room and walk towards the dark space, I wonder what I would let loose…

I am so very tired. I used to get through each day in here with the fear subdued. I know I have been in here so long, I have seen the passing of the days and felt the unwarranted gropes of my skin from the nurse more times than I care to remember. Her fingers were like crawling centipedes, trying to tickle above this flimsy gown. In truth, I could not have stopped her. I just hoped as she got towards the top of my thigh and lingered too long around my dried husk of a vagina that one of the spiders I let nestle in my womb, which I feed with the crusts of my memory, would skulk out and bite her, drag her into the pit and feast on her fingers, devour her breasts and then allow the children to bite and chew at the gristle of her remains.

She is a poor excuse for a woman. She doesn't care that she gets her kicks from abusing the sick and mentally ill, those of us in her care. I read once that the slaves who were entombed alive with the bodies of their pharaohs used to kiss and rub themselves on the engraved images of their once-glorious master's tombs. Whether this was out of devotion or finally getting to fuck them over, I don't know, but at least they had the courage to do it. This nurse, she goes so far and then stops, as if the electricity she's feeling has become too shocking, that she brings herself to the point of orgasm and then dies down below. She doesn't just do it with me; she has touched everybody in here except the new boss. Perhaps he is just too alive for her to cope with…

I don't want to do this anymore, the light is too bright, and there are weeds in my garden. I must attend to them.

Why are you doing this? I overheard you say to him that you were getting close. Close to what? Close to me? Close to a truth of what has happened in my life? Let me spell it out for you: I am the daughter of a murderess, I was a junkie once, loved the thrill of the drug as it coursed through my veins. My regret was that my husband and my father-in-law should not have witnessed what I was becoming. After that, I didn't really care anymore.

Now you have dredged these memories up, you have made me grieve for a boy I hardly knew. You have put ideas into my mind, you have taken away my view from my cottage. What for? Am I a guinea pig? My mind is on display, and you get to see me squirm in the drains? When this is over, when you have got what you need, are you going to go further than the nurse? Are you going to bring yourself to the point of ecstasy as you shuffle back and forth on the tape recordings, a couple of strokes and you flopping back in your chair, sated, breathing heavy, your pulse no longer beating out in time with the blood building up? Will I be the fantasy woman that brings you to extreme pleasure as you relive raping my mind every day?

I'm not shouting, I'm not shouting, I don't like shouting…

***

One last visit…really, you have everything you need.

That solution looks different. There is no need to smile and shake your head. I may be insane but I'm not stupid. I wasn't always mad. Just because the kids didn't like coming to my house… They called me names, you know. The spiders made them scared of me. They terrified my mother, too—everybody was scared of me until one man saw past my weird affection for the spiders.

I have kept something back from you. I have kept a story hidden, and now I think you won't get to hear it. You're putting me back in my cottage now, aren't you?

You're going to tell people that your tests, whilst encouraging, showed no discernible improvement in the long term. You have used me, you have put a wilderness of new homes, rabbit hutches and thousands of screaming children in the way of my view, that railway line, that closed off tunnel, the bugs—for what?

My eyes are heavy, but I have a tale for you, I have a confession. I think I caused my mother to kill my father. I think she put that knife in his neck because she wanted to kill me but knew what the outcome would be. All those times she told people there was nothing wrong with her eye when a black dark bruise appeared, she put it there. The scars on her wrists—she did that. The bite marks—she was the one who put her teeth to her skin and then blamed it all on my dad.

That knife, I think that was for me because I finally realised what was going on—that she hated him, that she feared me—and when it all got too much for her, what better than making a scene, waiting for me to come into the kitchen to check out the noise and commotion, and then plunging the knife straight into the neck of the man she had abused by stealth for years?

She got her own way. Hanging of women was abolished, and she could claim years of spousal abuse. She had every excuse under the sun, and she had a way to finally get rid of me. It was almost planned perfectly—what could I do? Testify my concerns? Speak up against my mother? All I could do was hate her, as I know I am going to hate you for what remains of my life. If that was poison dripping from the needle, if the syringe contained the means to shut me up quickly, I'm guessing it would have done so by now. So if the plan is to let me sleep again, then go. You have done your job. I have talked and remembered.

Let me tell you now: I am gone. I am wasted, and after today, I will not speak again. My story is over; and why? Because I have lost faith in it all. I will tell you all I want you to know and then that is it; you can all join me in hell.

19.

A Tale of the Shot in the Dark

IT WAS FAR from over. The sound of the emergency services rang with clarity above the rumble of my friend's home slowly crumbling into dust. Smoke and splinters of debris shifted and danced in the Maltese night. I looked down at the body of a man I had called brother, who had helped me overcome one of the greatest hurdles of my life, who, in his final moments, tried to protect me one last time.

I had removed from his blood-soaked fingers the file he had fought to preserve from the fire, that he'd taken a bullet for and died defending. In my experience, people only did that when they wanted something to be put right, a distress flare of guilt dispelled and thrown into the wind for all to see. Nobody ever truly leaves a secret to die with them.

The three of us remaining stood alert at the bottom of the garden as firefighters fought expertly to control the red hot flames and crumbling of walls and memories. I heard my driver over the radio several times during the couple of hours it took for it to become safe enough Aakster and I to gingerly make our way past the remains of what was once a home fit for a prince of poetry. I say I heard—what came across was muffled and full of static broken up by the sirens and an ambulance taking away the body of the policeman left at the gate. I pieced together that one of the three yacht owners I had arrested earlier that evening had been released. He had a good lawyer, one I had tried on many occasions to detain on the grounds of bribery and collusion. He had managed to provide documents asserting his clients whereabouts, and my superior had caved completely.

He was working on the second yacht owner, and I figured, by the time I was released from the back-garden open prison, with the sound of gushing water in front of me, the crash of waves chowing down on smoke and dreams behind me, that man would also be as free as the day he bought his first car.

What interested me, though, was the third man. When I enquired about him, my driver told me he was sitting tight. He wanted to talk to the officer who had arrested him earlier that evening. *That evening…* I looked at my watch when I heard those words and raised my eyebrows as I confirmed the time with my colleague. Nearly one in the morning; Time had been relentless. It had moved with the agility of a back-alley cat caught momentarily in the beams of a car and had disappeared into the coal-black hell whence it came before the driver even blinked. In the course of a few hours, the world had gone in pursuit of that cat, believing it was running after a kindly but slightly obscure white rabbit with a timepiece in its paw, declaring with pompous agitation that it was late, ever so late.

Time was as it always had been. I had been behind on the case from the beginning, only catching glimpses of the rabbit and the mask it wore at certain moments, peeling back the layers and the ruff-fur like a glove. If Time was presenting itself in such a manner then I was watching it under the delusion of one who had contracted myxomatosis. Death was inevitable wherever the shadow behind it all was standing. I had the pictures from the CCTV in the facility; I had the sworn statement from the manager, and I had the doctor's mother's body in the morgue at the nearest hospital. She had company—the man who had been duped into helping the so-called professor and his thin-faced accomplice who'd hanged himself two days before. Everywhere the tentacles of this man reached out, the result was the same: death was the winner.

Death was becoming a habit. I felt the rush of the chase—a feeling I had long since discarded when I came to my senses over the path I was taking. I had been in control for so long, not even she, that viper in my own nest, had managed to stir the hatred and bile in me to the point where I had drawn my gun and almost driven home into the brain of a strung-out junkie. But this man was pure evil. If I failed to finish this, he would regain a foothold on the island and the whole narcotics cycle would inevitably start again.

We left the remaining policeman in possession of my friend; this once I didn't think he'd mind me walking out on him. I bent down one last time, and with the file he had saved from the fire tucked underneath my arm, I gently patted him on the back. As gestures went, it was not much, but what was I to do? I could raise a glass to him later; if this was resolved without much more fuss, I could get drunk in The Pub while the owner and I swapped tales and built him to be a man of fine valour when really and truly, in many ways, he was a heel and a scoundrel. Yet the women loved him, my parents thought he was the bee's knees, and I, deep down, loved him like no other person on Earth.

The driver had come as close to the mess of vehicles and activity as he could. Further down the road, a couple of houses now had their lights on. When all this was over, I planned to come back to those houses and ask the owners outright what they had seen, why they had not called for help. I knew the questions would be met with a wall of silence; everybody had their price, and for a lot of people in this case, the price was very high.

We sped through the narrow lanes that surrounded the area and came out quickly into the main conurbation, the relentless build-up of houses, apartments and concrete. There was no escaping this, even at the north end of the island where once the beach at Mellieha Bay stood vast and beautiful as you approached her from the downhill curve that passed the Triq Il-Marfa;

now, holiday complexes and souvenir shops blocked the view. Everywhere I looked, my island was becoming a housing estate, an endless network of built-up fortunes making the economy boom and bust with equal pleasure.

The driver went with assured speed all the way back to the station. Very little passed between the three of us, but every so often, I heard Aakster mutter words of frustrated, futile encouragement, of impatience to get there before the third man was released. My mind was elsewhere, desperately trying to take in what seemed like my friend's last will, words that made no sense, an admission of guilt far worse than that to which he would have confessed if his wits had not been dealt several blows in the last few days.

Was he going to hand this all over? Was it even intended for me? The thought went through my racing mind that he only saved this file to have something to hold onto, the measure of his sins that made him the man he never wanted to be. I knew so little of his life before the island that I sometimes forgot he'd had one, secretive and guarded, before he came into my world; our world. I closed the file. This information, the revelation, was for later, and whilst it had bearing, I had other things to consider.

We pulled up outside headquarters just as the smarm and greasy hands of bribery and coercion were being oiled. With a smile that only a shark's mother could love stood a man I could quite happily see hang stark naked from the top of Triton Fountain and pay a few of the locals of Valletta and Floriana to throw stones and insults at him. Hell, I would join in and then arrest him for vagrancy.

His smile beamed broadly when he saw me get out the car. It was almost bursting at the sides, and I felt like I was no longer bait but the fish despairingly pulling on the end of the line, tiring myself out as he played and toyed with me. As I pushed past, he shouted out it was time for me to call it a day. Several high-profile murders, a beloved lecturer and man of the island dead at the hands of terrorists…

"What next, Inspector?" he bellowed. "Resign for the sake of the safety of the people of Malta."

I stopped and looked at him, his small, shallow face puffed up with ego and venom. His eyes cold, remorseless, a snake in the path of paradise. I felt my blood boil for the third time in just a few hours—thankfully, my colleague stepped in. She pushed me on, towards the group of reporters, social media exploiters, with the calm assurance a police officer is supposed to have. A brawl in the street with a lawyer was not going to help anybody or the situation that was close to exploding before our eyes.

I made my way past the mouths and the cameras, the thought of answering any questions far from my mind. From behind me, I heard the sleazy brick tones of the lawyer once more, telling me the game for me was over; by the following day, everybody would be calling for my resignation.

"Go back to your firework displays, Inspector."

I turned on my heel so quickly I only just caught sight of two people coming through the doors in front of me: a young woman and one of the men I had arrested earlier. Against my express wishes and her concerns, they had let both go. She'd warned us that to do so would be suicide. I scanned quickly around; nobody I didn't recognise; the scourge of the press and social media reporting world all in attendance.

Something was wrong. This was too perfect. I looked to my colleague and saw in her eyes the same escalating fear that something was going to give. We were both overwrought—was my paranoia only based upon the growing tenseness of the conclusion, the end game? I had watched my friend die, his house and yacht burned and destroyed, lit alight as if they were but toys, symbols of a desire to wipe every trace of the man off the island.

I had been living off a state of nerves since the day I realised the man I met in London all those years ago was back. I was near frazzled, burnt out like a study under attack, nerves and hallucination brought on by gulping in rancid smoke and the pressure of death that was creeping ever onwards.

The two accessories to the whole case passed me, one almost nonchalantly, a sideways glance with *I shall be overjoyed to see you suffer* etched deep into his fading glory eyes, the other's darting with ferocity, her nerves just as shot as mine, her other senses heightened.

Again, the lawyer shouted out, seemingly making a joke at my expense. Aakster was losing her rag. Her six foot frame had intimidated many of those she had come across in the relatively short time she had been on the island, yet that lawyer—at least five inches shorter than she—continued smiling as the night crept closer to the witching hour. He stood on tiptoes and whispered in her ear, her reaction alerting me too late to how the day would end.

The shot in the dark—it is always the one that catches you unawares. The sound sharp, invisible and full, it crackles like electricity, its target unseen but one you have less chance of surviving. Everybody panics; some stand still, their thought being that if the aim is true then by ducking they just add to the confusion. After all, why would someone target a member of the press?

The first shot zipped past me on my right side, and a scream became a thud on the floor. I felt the whisper of death, and it sounded like a dog whistle in my ears, a high-pitched, piercing murmur saying *you next*, the gossip of a projectile deciding whether you lived or died. My eyes gravitated towards the two people closest to me, sharp as the bullet, a whisper of my own, groping for signs that they were alive.

The girl was dead, the bullet finding her as sure as she had an arrow pointing to her brain, a slight sigh of life plucked from nothing, a whisper.

A second bullet sliced the air, a snapshot, the camera flash with powered speed. Not so much a whisper this time, the bullet caught the boat owner straight in the throat.

I shouted to Aakster to keep her eyes peeled. This was going to end with more people dying this night, I was sure…never have I been more relieved to be wrong. Two shots, one person dead, the other hanging on but surely gasping his last as spurts of blood spotted and mingled with the now tainted air.

This had all been planned. I looked to the lawyer, standing perfectly still and calm, measured, composed, as though he had just ordered a cup of tea in a fashionable London café. Two shots in the dark and he hadn't even broken a sweat; not a ripple had stirred. He smiled, and then, without a care in the world, he picked up his briefcase and strolled off towards his expensive car, leaving the two people he had managed to free from the cells on the cold floor, the natural commotion kissing his wheels as he drove away.

All hell broke loose around me. Shouts, a couple of women screamed, one young man fell at my feet, his Dictaphone cracking on the hard, blood-splattered floor. Officers ran to control the scene, cameras flashing, the digital print and proof of the events surely now going to make early morning risers on social media choke and rant as they read a one-sided story that had once again taken a turn for the worse.

Worse—how could it be worse? This was an evening in my life that I would never have imagined. My sister's drowning had been devastating, but this was torture, misery I had married, torment I had claimed in the last few hours as the spoils of war.

Aakster rushed over to me, shoving her way through the throng of people. She grabbed me by the hand and pushed me towards the station doors, out of the glare of the limelight the gunman had created and into the fluorescent brilliance of false harsh light. She touched my face, and in a fit of claustrophobia I pushed her away. I swore at her, asking what the lawyer had said to make her duck, to shrink like a coward in the face of the threat at hand.

Still, she tried to hold my head. She reached out roughly, and this time I allowed it. She studied my forehead and breathed a deep sigh of relief as she proclaimed that it was a superficial graze, some stitches perhaps, and it certainly needed cleaning, but otherwise no serious damage.

"Don't worry," she urged. In my paranoid state, I thought she was implying I had been the target, that the poor girl who took a bullet to the brain was a secondary concern, that despite telling us very little, she had paid the price because of a slight variation in degrees and the stiff air that separated the gun and my hide.

Aakster took me by the hand again and led me to my desk, forcing me to sit on my faded leather chair. She shouted out for someone to get a cup of tea, failing that, a stiff drink, naming a brand I was particularly fond off. I looked into those Dutch eyes and wondered how I had never before had a colleague who instinctively knew what to do, to take charge. It came with a different mentality, I guess. She was excellent at her job, and not for the first time, I realised how much I was going to miss her.

Quickly and calmly, she told me what had happened in the moments leading up to the deaths on our doorstep, the simple message from the lawyer that she was told to convey to me. My throat went tight, and she forced me to drink, so dry, trembling at the enormity of it all. I didn't know what was in my friend's file, but in my heart I knew all the death, all the chaos that had befallen my island was, to all intents, my fault.

A young woman came across with a first-aid kit and insisted, quite vocally, that I needed to go to hospital. There was too much to do; I needed to finish this, and I had less than twenty hours to make sense of what was missing from the case. I asked Aakster if she would interview the remaining boat owner, and she confirmed, somewhat oddly, that it would be a pleasure. I opened the file and started to read as the young woman wiped the remains of the blood from my temple.

20.

The Tale of the Spider (As Told to a Lawyer)

I WAS AT THE heart of it all, until things became somewhat aggressively out of hand. Trusting the wrong person can lead you to being removed—so much better to have them taken out first, cleaned from the evidence chain.

I would offer you a glass of brandy, but I hear you're teetotal. I don't trust that. It isn't seemly, gentlemanly, to refuse a glass of something special when conducting business or confessing one's sins. However, I shall overlook it, for you are charging me a lot of money for this show, and it is spectacular, a three- or even four-ringed circus, one where some people will need to be wiped in order for me to resurface as part of a once proud society.

Heroin—that was the game, and what a game it was! You're too young to remember what it was like, dealing in timetables, shipments, potatoes...yes, potatoes. I had a farmer on the island paid to turn his whole yearly crop over to me, and we fashioned a perfect solution for getting the merchandise from Africa to Europe right here in the middle, caught between the Devil, the deep-blue sea and the forgotten and misused continent. I was making a killing.

I have never liked the image of the Devil, shades of hypocrisy strewn all the way through it, so black and white. Do one bad thing and you must be evil; do a million good things on top, and still everybody labels you as being in league with Satan. I think that's why I deeply enjoyed basing my production and office here on this deeply Catholic island; the irony of God-fearing people always on the lookout for anything that might taint their community amused me. Now, you see thousands upon thousands of visitors come here, soak up the sun, play around a little, cheat and get drunk, sweat and fuck like it's going out of fashion. OK, it's not as bad as the islands off Spain, but the Brits that go there are not my kind of people. Pompous, arrogant, full of swagger and piss, they strut about as if they own the place. They are a relic of memory, of soldiers invading country after country in the name of a forgotten and damned empire.

My father disliked them. He did business with them during the war…married one. I disliked her as much as I admired him. Ruthless, he was. Part of a great dynasty of traders, buyers, purchasers. Any man can be bought, he taught me. You just have to offer him something he desperately craves; it was my honour to take his life at the end when he'd taught me all that he knew.

The Devil—what a waste of symbolism. It is man that is the horned one, always taking, destroying the Earth, and what for? To grow fat, to lose the will to fight for what is right, to praise the species on two legs, four or even the Ankabūt; to wield power over nature. It is no wonder, my friend, that people such as I exploit that greed, turn them against themselves and make them as sick as the ground they walk on.

Or I did. I used to, until I was finally caught because I trusted the wrong man, a boy.

I was fond of him, you know. He was keen, intelligent…and easily manipulated due to his relationship with his father. I gave him a glimpse of the world and he revelled in it. For a while, anyway. Then he met that insufferable little bastard from England, a boy who would grow up to be a big man on the island—that little shit took my position, and his only vice was for the women.

Did I tell you how easy it was to pull the strings of the one woman who had slept with both the detective and the doctor? What a fine thing, what sport! Pretending to care for her, listening as she slammed them both—the doctor's love of the young woman who had usurped her position in his bed and the detective's unwillingness to be the man she wanted him to be. Oh, she was a bitch all right, couldn't stop her mouth from rattling on once she got going. It was an absolute pleasure to listen to her tales and even nicer to slit her throat as she lay on her bed waiting for me to listen some more. I thought about framing both of them for that. It would not have been impossible, I am a man with influence, after all. Even now, less than a year out of prison, and already this Ankabūt is capable of weaving webs to catch many flies.

Appeal to a person's vanity and they soon fall in line. The doctor with the young student, oh, so enamoured by his work, fawning at his pen, his thoughts. The young woman, found on the streets of Liverpool, a perfect decoy as she stood there—I introduced her as my daughter, right there in his office, her grades manufactured, a piece of pie with which to lure him, the silk thread tingling in the air—she was too easy. Money in the bank, a chance to escape what she had put herself through; now released, in heaven or hell, dancing with the good doctor in the middle of my web.

As I stood in his office, surrounded by his damn books and his easy charm, I wanted to kill him there and then. It would have saved time, but where is the drama in that? He had to suffer, he had to fall, for his arrogance, for the quarter of a million pounds' worth of heroin he sent to the bottom of the sea as a boy. Better he suffer, and what a way to send him down. Kill his mother, kill his former lover, get his girlfriend to be part of a plot to lose his job, his respect, his fucking beloved yacht and finally his life.

It was a nice touch, by the way, blowing the house up. I liked that house, clean, tidy, any other man and I would have made sure there was not a single mark on the building, not a single bullet hole.

That policeman on the gate…that was a mistake. I'm going to have to explain that to some people when this is over tomorrow. But still, omelettes and all that.

She was special, you know, his mother. Like all the members of her sex, she was despicable to me, but I found her interesting. In another life, I dare say I would have enjoyed her company; I would have found her thoughts on spiders particularly illuminating. It comes down to control, doesn't it? The right substance to bring someone out of their stupor, the correct dosage with which to make their mind alert, then just as easily snap it shut. I took great pleasure hearing the desperation in that funny little man's voice as he spoke quickly down the phone, as he told me that she had repeatedly smashed her head against the wall of her room until the banks burst in her mind, and her brain, the images that had not been tainted by her guilt or by our actions, smeared and ran down the wall.

I wonder what her last thoughts were? She was wrapped up completely in that fantasy world. Her garden, her bloody garden, always cropping up when we brought her out of her self-induced stupor. That tunnel, too—I can only surmise that she was somehow remembering the night she decided to put a needle in her son, that dark and dingy place where they found her, strung out, skin on bones and cobwebs. I can only hope that it all fell to pieces. We nearly lost her once—too much dosage, too much memory—we could have been discovered at that point. It was a good idea to keep away for a few days; it gave her time to focus on the pain again.

Pain—that is what drives everything in the world. Want to be famous? It is the pain of neglect from your parents. Can't handle the modern world? That's the pain of your conscience talking for not fighting back against the rapid tide and the rubbing hands of fascists and the dyed-in-the-wool liberal elite as they fight endlessly over how to control the masses.

Pain—I raise a glass to it, I salute it, for without it we have no idea what we are capable of achieving in life. We have no mastery over the inner voice saying *give in, give in, give in*.

Pain is what becomes of us when we allow ourselves to wallow in its fruitlessness, its damage and the nerves that are frayed beyond final measure.

Pain is exactly what I believe our good inspector is feeling right now. The shock of the last few hours will push him to the edge. I suspect that even now, he is contemplating his final moments. He knows I will kill him, that this is all about revenge on the two boys who ruined me, who put me in jail. So much I have missed, so much I had to watch from the sidelines as I rotted in that fucking jail, whilst the one who sank a shipment of pure heroin becomes a doctor of a paltry language—an abuse to the tongue—and the other, in irony of ironies, becomes a man of law. The boy who betrayed me completely is now the seemingly respectable man behind a badge.

Pain—one dead, one to go, and all those little pieces in between silenced, paid off or so frightened they will be looking over their shoulder for the rest of their lives.

Oh, it is good to be back here, my friend. I am going to love my retirement. Perhaps prison wasn't a bad thing in some respects; it gave me time to think; it gave me time to plan. It also gave me a chance to regroup, for the fall of the Afghan market was a suitable response to that day when two sons of Babel fell. Their loss brought pain to the Eastern world; by inflicting pain, pain was doubled, trebled, quadrupled, and I got it all back at rock-bottom prices.

Raise a glass, my friend, for tomorrow night, all this will be over. I have so much longed for this day. The doctor was incidental, an amusement with which to take the smug little prick down. Did you ever read any of his work? Unintelligible, cheap university applause in the guise of fawning. When I think of the English tongue, normally it is reserved for whores and prostitutes, the cheap toilet gag and the theft of rich language from that vile race of invaders. Sir Walter Raleigh was nothing more than a jumped-up pirate yet he was praised for his verse—I would have hanged him for both acts of treachery.

How is the Dutch girl? Suitably scared, I hope. I remember her; I remember a lost little girl in the shadow of a great man. I was younger then, not fresh or green but building my own portfolio of great works. Her aunt was a precious flower plucked before her time, an easy addict, no love from her parents, her father a war hero who had faced too many bullets and told too many lies to stay alive. I admired him somewhat; he was a man of action—quiet, determined—it was a pleasure to take his hand, fuck his daughter and snap her will as easy as it was straightforward to snap a Nazi neck in an alleyway or blow up a supply route to the frontline. I admired him, but he was so cold towards his family, always hiding things. Rescuing a Jewish woman, that took guts, I admit, but keeping a weapon hidden in his shed? Only a madman would think his granddaughter would not explore and would believe her idol when he told her he got rid of the weapon.

Pain, my friend, makes us do silly things. It makes us say monumentally stupid things at times when it would be better to stay quiet and be thought a cynical, comfortable fool. That hero came to me and offered me his pride and joy, and by doing so sealed his own fate. He offered me that gun, told me his granddaughter had found it hidden and he could no longer trust himself to keep it around. His granddaughter, sweet Aakster… how I enjoyed giving him above the price for the weapon of his war so that it would pay for her eventual schooling. Her time was not wasted, I see.

You look tired, my friend. The evening's excitement is finally catching up with you. You lawyers—you are all the same. You think too much, and you get paid for the privilege of it, yet you only have the heart for the fight if it involves legal speak and scoring points over the justice system. You're like actors, in a way. You learn the lines, you dress for the occasion and then you move on. Another show in another town, playing to the gallery—I hate you all, but you prove yourselves to be useful every so often.

I rather enjoyed taking that shot tonight, the one at the girl, my daughter, my stooge. The boat man—what was he worth? Just like the doctor, he was an added bonus. Very much like the detective's wife, she had become tiresome, a pain in my neck, the poisoned thorn in my side. Her plans were tedious, no imagination. The wanton whore. She love me, she said. "Tell me you love me," she kept demanding. Anybody can tell someone they love them, but it takes true love to let them go, and an obsession with the job at hand to slaughter them as they sleep.

That job is nearly complete; the work is nearly over, and soon, it will be playtime once again. There is an empire to rebuild, and I am still young. There is a fresh opportunity in the world. People are tired, they are in pain, and where there is pain, there is suffering, and where that exists it is only right to supply medicine, to offer a solution. Death is a means to an end, but before that, you should never let the misery of existence drag you down.

Think about it, my friend. There are wars everywhere, gang wars into which innocents get dragged, world wars from which the innocent cannot escape. The skyline of a city changed forever because of backhanders and feverish corruption. People lose their jobs; they see bleakness and the dark creeping up on them as if they are caught in a terrifying scene in a jungle. Through the evening mist, they see eyes, sharp and piercing. They hear noises and start to imagine the worst. In their panic, their hearts starts to pound, to quiver, to beat quicker; their breathing becomes erratic, and soon they believe their heart will give out, and for what? The tiger didn't move a muscle; the gorilla paid no interest. It was the scurrying of spiders that finally made them pass out and die.

I have enjoyed this. All that time in prison was worth it. Fuck with me, destroy a million-pound cargo, screw with me by deceiving me. It is a game at the end of the day, a simple game, about which the tiger never worries and the gorilla could not give a damn. But the spider…that spider weaves and is patient.

The bigger the spider, the more frightening it looks as you rush along through the jungle and get caught up in webs and half-dissolved flies that stick to your face and get in your eyes and throat. It is a game of patience; the winner is never the tiger or gorilla—they are too close to the needs of man—it is the stealthy spider, hiding in the corner, occasionally coming out to hunt in the shifting light, content to sit there until the fly comes to him. The tiger may have jaws and speed, the gorilla will beat its chest and has more strength in its arms than a vice, but a spider has cunning and fangs, and from these fangs drips poison.

Pain—we are all in pain, my learned friend. We all require something extra to make us believe we can elevate ourselves above the clouds for a while, that we might see the point of tomorrow with wars, poverty and ignorance to get in our way. But soon we come down to Earth with such force that our brains spill out of our ears and our reason takes a tumble. It is for that the spider waits. It watches us fall like Icarus and while our wings burn, it will gently start to put our soul inside its web, forever dissolving, forever dying.

Drink up. I need rest before tomorrow. You have to work on getting rid of the other boat owner…already taken care of? Really? You are worth your weight in gold.

21.

The Tale of a Second Guy Fawkes

I READ THE FILE for the next hour and a half—my friend's life of symbolic misery and rejection, all measured and paced by one simple act after another, from neglect and near infanticide as a baby through to the terror of being passed around a system that didn't care—no wonder the boy ran away. I admired his courage, I felt sickened by the despair, I was surprised by his words, and in the end, when I closed the file and put it in my desk drawer, slowly turning the key and locking it away from other eyes, I felt almost more exhausted than I had ever done in my life…not quite, but almost.

I could see his shame in mine, and yet he was filled with a yearning to be free and be someone of his own value, someone the world might respect even if he could not live up to the hype of his engineering. Me, I hid behind a badge and once upon a time behind my own father's uniform, his gallantry. I concealed myself in the dark and went undercover as an honourable man. I married a good-looking woman; I had a son; I won awards and citations. The clean policeman, they once called me. If I survived the next day, all that would change. I would be put on the fire like a Guy Fawkes effigy. First, I would singe as the fire closed in, then, with a whoosh, I would be caught in the glare of an inferno, smoke billowing outwards and choking my screams. My career was over; best to go out in that blaze of glory.

My eyes had seen too much in the last few hours, more than a man should see, but it was all of my own making. The connections had been woven together from the start. My fate was a strand, a silk line that had been placed with mathematic ingenuity and was as strong a link to the spider's mouth as it ever had been. I disliked spiders; I was starting to realise why.

If I had not gone to that bonfire night in London, perhaps my part in this would never have happened. I could have gone into the fight for my life prepared to die an honourable death, but then, I only became a policeman because of that day, the sight of a burning symbol, the smell of chestnuts and potatoes fighting for supremacy amid the acrid aftertaste of fireworks urged to fly into the cold London air, the flames leaping from one stick to another, from collected branch to bundles of stuffed and rolled newspaper, the pictures on the front and gossip columns inside only fit for the fire on the green.

I was transfixed. I was on my own in a foreign city, and I was seeing a different side to life, the flames dancing, bickering and snapping at each other in the second that they existed. Children carried sparklers, making them move with exotic intent—a couple of years later in life and I would have sought a different, more seedy kind of exoticism in London, the dancing flames onstage who slowly dropped their skirts and removed their underwear as they were whistled and cheered on by businessmen and their crowded, jugular-throated companions. A bonfire would have to do, the burning man in the middle a poor substitute for the prospect of seeing the heat in another place.

Out of the shadows, traced by the outline of a child's sparkler, emerged a conjured devil in a sharp suit out of place amongst the warm scarves and playful descent into the realms of British history. He sat down beside me and offered me conversation and a plastic pint glass filled with a syrupy, undisclosed make of beer. We talked, me wearily at first, he with an air of supreme confidence and gentle ease. He asked if I was enjoying the spectacle, the show, the sense of occasion. I could barely see his face, only the semi-captured outline that briefly glimmered as the fire burned and crackled when the flames found wet wood.

Fireworks—they are an illusion. They are the ejaculation of a thousand pounds spent in the hope of entertaining a mind for several minutes. They are the prelude and the aftermath to sex, so much build-up for a small set of bangs and then disappointment coming over you in waves straight after. When I look back now at the money spent celebrating, commemorating an event that was all over the disagreement of politics and religion, my stomach turns. All right, celebrate and make merry the start of a new year, the countdown of the old. Light up a job lot of gunpowder and let it flare in the sky, let it add stars to a full cosmos. But really, a date which nobody now can forget because they subconsciously want to score points over a friend? Time and fireworks: the perfect match in the illusionary heavens.

He impressed me with his knowledge of Malta. He had friends there, he said, a small business venture—did I like chips? What teenage boy doesn't. He had access to the best chips—a small farm on Malta grew the best potatoes around. He mentioned the farm; I knew of it. You get to know everybody eventually.

The night drew onwards, the smoke beguiling as it flirted with the Thames mist, the heady cocktail of burning embers and ghosts plunged into the depths of the dirty river and rising ready to take vengeance in ethereal form. The conversation never faltered, only stopping as the applause went up for what had been a great show of childish military strength. The man stood up and offered me his hand, his grip ice cold, bony, splintered, like shards of steel. A chill went through me, a foretelling perhaps, the memory to come passed down in the gesture of the ages. *Trust me*, it said, and like the reckless child holding a sparkler too close to composition of magnesium, ferrotitanium, devil's sulphur and the ever popular charcoal, I could not wait to feel the heat beneath my hands, knowing I would be burnt.

Foretelling—I disagree with that. Perhaps just a feeling, a sense of death or unease that comes to us all when confronted by an offer from a devil. Whatever your belief, I had fallen straight into the trap. I had gone giddy with the stories of the man's life—all lies. I know that now, but at the time, I was a child in long trousers, impressionable, willing to see the world as a playground stuffed with swings and roundabouts. There is always the urge to rebel when you are the son of a policeman; you tend to either be so uptight that you die of insufferable snitching or you blow like a volcano and send so much rage into the sky you destroy everything around you. I was torn always between the two, it seems.

We met twice more during those few days my family were in London: a great place; a city that sealed my fate.

What did we talk of? It seemed innocent; it still does, if I think about it. The conversation always turned to the island—what a great place it was to grow up, to feel the sun on your back and the pleasure of the water under your feet. Island life is idyllic. It is also hard and dangerous. You are at the mercy of the sea, but nobody tells you this when you think of moving there. Nobody suggests anything but the peace and tranquillity, the old-fashioned neighbourly tradition, no locked doors, everybody saying hello. This is the picture postcard every island race wants you to see, because the downside of living in paradise is that there is no money to invest. *Why do you need to repair that church? It looks so quaint!* Well, stranger, it is crumbling piece by holy piece, because you allowed a nation built upon nationalistic steroids and fevered antisocial beliefs to bomb us too shreds, but please take home a few memories and over-the-limit packets of cigarettes.

I am cynical on some things; modern expression is one—the need for everything to be filmed, put out to the world, every mistake, every false start demonised and allowed to pull a person down. It does nothing for me, and I am glad I made my biggest mistakes before the invention of smart phones and the corrosive internet. Imagine trying to steal guns from a farm now. Think for a minute what it would take for someone to film without permission an event that ends in tragedy. Surely it is bad enough, horrific enough to witness as one person, your eyes forever seeing a young girl lose her hand in a trap, a rusty snare that you know had been set out for you.

Now, it would be all around the world in a few minutes, the shock on a mother's face as she pleads with her husband to get the girl free but knowing, deep down, the best that might happen is the girl will lose a lot of blood and be dangerously ill for some time.

Perhaps I am cynical, or perhaps I see the destructive power in something so tiny, so insidious. My dead friend could have been a little more distrusting of the modern world as he took his last breath. So many dead, that poor girl amongst them.

We look back at the past with fondness, mostly. I had a fairly good childhood; I once had a loving sister; I was once seriously thinking of doing anything but police work. We look back with fondness at the shower of colours coming down to Earth from an explosive display of fireworks because the other option is to understand that we have been mugged by the future, that our path from one simple handshake wakes the impending events, and we hear its hungry growl.

That handshake so long ago put my future on red alert. It was starving; now, it grinds its teeth in anticipation of the meal finally being presented and the bones that will go into the finger bowl. I read a story once by an American author, a horror, psychological, perhaps not his best story, but when you write so many, the details of what sells are immaterial. In this tale, Time was a beast. It had teeth, it was ever starving, and if you got left behind for even a second, it would catch you and strip you out of existence like a piranha taking down a cow in trouble in the water. Time has teeth; my Time has waited with patience, and all it cost me was that handshake in the dark...always meeting in the dark with the fear that I was talking to the dead.

Where do you go when you willingly courier a small parcel back to the island with a couple of hundred pounds in your pocket for your trouble? The only way is further into the web. No one would stop you—a small trinket for a friend, but to pay tax would defeat the object, he told me with sincerity. An address was given, memorised and then burned; money was exchanged. *Nobody will stop you. You are the son of a policeman. You have the eyes of trust upon you.*

That third time when he asked me to do him a favour, that was my get-out clause. There was the chance offered to me by Time and tide: *get out now.* I didn't take it, and look where it has led me. Straight to the jaws. I can almost smell its hunger; I can taste its victory. I have screwed up, and not even my father can save me this time.

Take the parcel to Malta, hang around on a street corner or two, pass this message along to the woman in the red skirt and holding the camera. Clean my car for me, get the blood stain out. A bit of money here, a sum of silver there...Time has long memories, patient bastard that it is.

The final moment before the rug was pulled on my ever-increasing damnation was to go to the farm. The farmer was losing his nerve and possibly his marbles. He had become secretive, unhelpful; he was walking towards blowing the operation, and whilst I had no clue what they were talking about, I guessed this was the place where the buck always landed.

If I had known from the start they were dealing in heroin on that farm, I would have kept well away. I would never have talked to the man in the first place, would never have allowed myself to fall for the charm and the stories. The sparkler always looks beautiful, it throws illumination onto the night sky, but it is an illusion. It can no more power a home than it can a Christmas tree, but it can burn and tear a mother's love to pieces.

From a handshake to seeing a little girl lose her hand. What choice did I have? Something inside me snapped back into reality. I was not the person I was becoming. I was a good lad; I am a good man. My friend made me see that. He was good to me after the event, after my father partially disowned me, banished me to service in a restaurant where I worked until I bled. I wish my friend had told me more about his life and saved me from reading the cold hard, cynical facts in a collection of notes and autographed confessions.

I feel myself nodding off. There is commotion around me, and it stirs me from the jaws for a moment. Outside, the day is getting light. The tunnels, though, will always be dark, ominous, foreboding.

I need a plan. I need to set this all down before I see him face-to-face, before I shake his hand one last time and allow the beast to kill me.

I am not sure how long I have been thinking, but when I look up, Aakster is standing in the doorway before me. She is on edge. The whole floor seems up in arms, and accusations are flying. I ask my colleague to tell me what is going on. The noise is overwhelming, and my nerves, which were already frayed to the point of setting off a bomb in my stomach, are now stretched as thin as they can go.

Through gritted teeth, she explains the turn of events whilst I have been deep in thought. Her questioning of the final witness, the one who asked not to be released, went well. He spilled all he knew; his guts had turned inside out and information had come forth easily. He even gave her names and places of a new site which had become of interest, not just shipping drugs but people.

I wondered why the place was in uproar if all this had been received with minimal fuss. The building was pandemonium, and over Aakster's shoulder, I saw a policeman being roughly handled, a young man, no more than twenty-five, so fresh to the force he looked as if he had not started shaving yet. Aakster tried to shout over the commotion, but I figured it out long before she managed to get down to the brutality of it all.

As Aakster had closed the interview to her satisfaction and had come to collect me to go over what she had learned, the young policeman on duty outside the interview room had gone in and, without warning, put a knife through the man's neck, killing him instantly.

The struggle continued, screams and shouts from those in my charge. This was a complete mess; who on earth was I to trust now? How deep was this all going to go? The last firework went through my mind—the only answer I was going to receive: I would never know.

You may call it foretelling; I call it experience. In the back of my mind, I knew the young policeman was going to explode. I shouted out in time for Aakster to hit the deck and find cover. Across the room, the policeman reached behind one of his fellow officers' backs and pulled his pistol from its holster. The movement was swift, the delivery of justice quick and damning. In that single dance step, he twirled around, put the gun to his mouth and pulled the trigger.

Time has teeth. The longer the wait for justice, the sharper those teeth become. I only hoped the five or so minutes between slitting a man's throat and taking your own life would see Time unprepared to brush down its best suit and order a good wine. I hoped for mercy. I hoped that it would swallow him down in one go.

22.

The Tale of the Reluctant Saboteur

TWO WEEKS I spent on the streets of Barcelona, and for those two weeks, I found myself running the gauntlet between watching the boats come into the docks and the port, hiding from prying, inquisitive eyes and looks of suspicion and mistrust, and the fear that, at any moment, someone was going to hold onto my arm and shout out: *Found him, the missing boy from Britain. Here is the liar, the cheat, the thief.*

For two weeks, I lived on my nerves and very little else, I washed in the rain and in the sea. I stole what I could from the vendors to stay alive. I slept on sand made hard by others' enjoyment during the heat of the day. To my shame, I robbed from those who paid little attention to their belongings, though I didn't take much. Some clothes, the odd note sticking out of a pocket, and a watch which was growing warm in the heat of the Barcelona sun. I didn't feel guilty about that one, as I found, when I tried to sell it later that day, I was not the only one pretending to be something I wasn't.

Barcelona is a marvellous city, beautiful and alluring, the type of city you would make love to if you could afford it, and yet, like many other places, it is unforgiving if you are poor, broke and on the run.

I watched with interest the boats coming in and out, the tide bringing people from all over—holidaymakers, tourists, football fans, islanders in search of dry land, criminals…it was that last section of society that interested me the most.

I figured I had a choice: I could stay another couple of weeks and try to steal enough money to make my way on a boat as a genuine passenger, but without legal documents, it would not be long before I was heading home. The sea, in this case, would be the last I would taste of the freedom I had come to enjoy despite being often cold and hungry. Or I could get aboard one of the boats I had observed and stow away. I wouldn't know where I was heading, but if I kept myself hidden for a couple of days, I was sure the islands of Spain would be the best place to start over again.

My choice was limited, but so was my time. The last couple of days I had been down at the beach, I had noticed the same two policemen trailing me, at a distance, never too close, but enough to make themselves visible. I wondered if my description had been circulated as one who was nothing more than a petty thief, a pickpocket. Admittedly, it was true, but it didn't mean I wanted to go to jail for it. More to the point, I didn't want to go back home.

I resolved that the next time I saw the boat I had been keeping an eye on, then that would be the time to go. Just jump into the cargo hold and stay there until it was time to make an escape, hopefully under the cover of darkness. If not, then hope they didn't have guns and that I wasn't too far from any shoreline. I had no idea where they were going, but they were always here within a couple of days, all well tanned and well drilled. It were almost as if they never truly stopped, always docking into port, always busy, the clock always ticking on, never forgiving.

My chance came, and without further incident from the local police, on the night of my fifteenth day in the city. The warm weather made the locals appreciate the apparent laziness of their hordes of visitors, induced by the sun and the cloudless sky. For me, it was just a sign that I might be able to slip aboard the hulk of a boat and get into the hold once they had finished loading whatever cargo they were transporting that day. It was an omen, a sign that worked out well, the stone in weight I had lost since leaving England, and with an athleticism that had betrayed me all the way through senior school, I was up the gangplank, over the side, past several large wooden crates marked 'potatoes' in black, stamped lettering and down in the hold before anyone noticed a blur.

I found some tarpaulin and dragged it into the corner of the over-filled hold and pulled it over me. For the next two hours, I kept still and quiet, never daring to move a muscle, not wanting to give the game away and only finally breathing out loud when I heard the engines start and the shaft of light from the opening died down and eventually faded away.

For two days, I remained hidden, not trusting my luck that I would not be discovered by one of the crew, not understanding the layout of the vessel. I was surrounded by crate upon crate of potatoes, of food I couldn't touch, and the temptation to find a way to sneak out of the hold and see where we were was great. Twice the boat stopped, the engines groaned and ground to a less than satisfying halt; twice I believed the gig was up. The worst that could happen was a toss-up between being thrown overboard alive for sport or killed immediately and then dumped at sea.

Twice we stopped for what seemed an eternity, twice I felt my pulse racing and my stomach growl. Twice I was sure they were going to come down into the hold and find me. It was only after the second time the engines restarted with a spluttering indecision that I saw, on the opposite side to where I had been under the cover of a smothering tarpaulin, a small sliver of light, a gap in the darkness that was not there before. I froze; my hunger declared it was a trap. Someone had seen me and decided to toy with my senses. They had offered me a way out, but I was like the mouse who sees no cat around and becomes less wary of being pounced upon, does not realise the smell of the morsel of cheese, the sight of filling its aching belly, is actually a spring-loaded death machine. I shrank back.

To whoever reads this—and, my dear friend, I hope you know what to do with all these notes and confessions I leave you—I am not brave enough for confrontation. Part of me knew that if I were even to step out of the shadows, this crypt in the corner I had nested in, then I would open myself up for possible capture. It was always on my mind and had begun to take over how I saw myself. From the furthest recesses of my home-spun plastic web, I waited five minutes; ten, fifteen…twenty minutes went past, and finally I saw a shadow scurry past the door and push it shut. The possible trap had been avoided, but there I still was, in the web, a couple of bits of bread left in my bag, some ham, matches and a lighter I had stolen from one of the gift shops that waved visitors in and then gratefully booted them out when they had taken enough money to pay for their own food that night.

I crept forward slowly and allowed the tarpaulin to fall off me, the shroud for now displaced, my cover deserting me. Taking advantage of the darkness, of the little air that was coming in from the cracks and the patched-up repairs that had been going on since the vessel was launched, I felt my body creak as the enforced stiffness which had taken hold began to silently scream as I unlocked my young but seemingly disgusted-by-the-adventure bones.

I still feel stiff in certain weathers, undeniable circumstances. I don't swim as often as I should for a man of my age. I love water, but actually messing about in it, immersing myself in its gaping jaws and allowing it to toss me from side to side as it chews my energy and cramps my blood… I would rather stay dry, safe, on board a boat, never again down deep in the hold. I had never once taken a car abroad. I could not sit waiting for the ferry to dock, watching the bow doors open. I don't like that sense of metallic enclosure.

My eyes had become used to the little light afforded through the slits in the metal, and whilst at that time I could honestly say I had never understood the complexity of navigation, I knew we had gone some distance. What I hadn't heard was the reason for the two stoppages along the way. I reasoned it wasn't the condition of the boat; she seemed sound, semi-reliable and desperate to do her duty. There had to be another reason. I looked over the boxes, fear ebbing away. My body may have been voluntarily paralysed for the time I had been on the boat but my mind had raced, hardly sleeping, snatching minutes here and there, always too aware that someone might come in.

I'd found myself thinking of the girl back home whose reputation I could not save until it was too late, my conscience crying out for hours to be heard. With each wave that struck the side of the boat, with each drop of sea that slowly rusted away with my resolve, I thought of her. I veered between utter shame and pointless recriminations; I asked her forgiveness and I raged at her for making me become this hermit crab in plastic sheeting, cold, exhausted and alone.

For the first time since I had been on the run, I made a big mistake. The little ones—stealing and shoplifting—at that time and still now, I mitigate by telling myself it was in the name of survival, that in the scheme of things, an apple I had taken it from a fruit stall and bitten into over the course of the day was nothing compared to the lunacy of the world. Small victories justified; I had survived so far. What I did in the hold after realising how worryingly cold I had become was the universe's way of telling me I had come so very far but I was still stupid. I was a little boy playing an old man's game.

Always keeping an ear out for the sound of an opening door, the footsteps of strange men on the deck as they carried out the dull and the routine... I felt like some poor creature in the Garden of Eden sensing there was forbidden fruit to be tasted, and up above at the wheel, God in all his dirty overalls, drenched with sea sweat and oil, was ready to expel me for being mildly curious and hungry.

The same crates I had dodged past on deck were all there below, some marked 'potatoes', some marked with Arabic lettering, some labelled 'fireworks', a few with exotic-named places and codes underneath. A stack of boxes at the far end by the door were labelled 'Valletta', along with a man's name and a crudely drawn imprint of a spider to its side. I tried to pick up the nearest one; it weighed a tonne. Whatever was inside was stuffed in there to bursting. I backed away from the spider's property and looked over some more. I found a smaller set of crates, easily lifted, took one over to the corner in which my own web had been made and, with careful silence, took the crate apart.

My mistake, in retrospect, was to feel cold, to remember I had matches and paper in my bag. If push came to shove, I could light a small fire; I could at least keep my hands warm. Following through with such childish thought is perhaps a thing you should grow out of. I remember once setting alight a school tie as I waved it in front of a small portable gas heater. It seemed a good idea at the time, a mark of rebellion. It earned me more than a slap around the ears and the condemnation of the junior school headmaster.

Thin wood hides treasure, but again, all I found was potatoes in a crate destined for Gozo. A crate of cold, lumpy potatoes. I stared at those fiendish clumps of earth-driven food and wondered what I could do with them. I had become used to stealing in the name of survival; putting clumps of odd-looking potatoes in my bag—that was another thing altogether. But I had lost all sense of reason, and a dozen of them went into my bag and stayed there despite the water and the destruction of this little Eden.

I started a fire, a small one, just enough to at least feel some warmth, and sat on a box and breathed for a while, not thinking of her or the journey. Instead, I thought about my friends, or those I had left, back in my home town, who had not deserted me for the fawning arse of a lad who had taken the girl's memory. For an hour, I dreamt whilst my eyes slowly rested. For the first time in weeks I was comfortable. Never trust that feeling, for the gods always have a way of making sure you are tested just once more before revealing their true intent, their purpose.

The boat came to a sudden juddering halt, and I heard the sound of smaller vessels, at least two, their engines ominous, dynamic and demanding authority. I got off my box, put my bag over my shoulders and moved over to the grills. Mixed language, some English, a little Italian and French, and what I thought was possibly Arabic, none of what they were shouting made sense. I strained my ears, and in failing to understand any more, I pushed over a couple of crates and climbed on top.

A third boat, slightly bigger, different engine sound, came closer, and I heard what I thought was a gunshot, but through the grills above me, I saw the red smoke of a flare rocketing into the sky. One man shouted close by to turn the boat around, another quickly rebuking him.

When God sees you, he will do so with blazing eyes and a thunderous roar. For all those who pray constantly to see him: it is something you do not want at all.

I shifted a little too close to the grill, the sound of wood on metal was too obvious, and God, in the guise of a thin-faced man with piercing eyes, saw me. He saw this wretched creature in his own paradise, and he roared in disgust. I was no Adam or Eve being evicted from their home; I was an insect, a Colorado beetle amongst the prized merchandise. I would not be allowed to live; I was to be crushed underfoot and thrown out as casually as one would dispose of an empty web.

Two eyes bore down on me so quickly that I fell the six feet to the bottom of the hold, crashing against other crates as I flailed and thrashed, a flapping fish in a net he could not see, the sound of boxes shifting under their own momentum, breaking open, contents scattering, and me rolling around towards the back of the hold. Bruised and caught, my only saving grace was the bag on my back. As I struggled to my feet, I felt the cold clutch of a devil pull me up by my neck and drag me along through the once-welcome light that might have offered this mouse food and up the stairs onto the deck.

Gasping for breath, I was thrown onto the floor, and the world and its wife suddenly found me the most perplexing sight. Voices were raised, a gun was pointed at me, and through tears of exhaustion and self-pity, I managed to raise my arms, imploring them not to shoot.

More shouts, a series of barked commands and orders, counter-demands, the sound of the sea bashing against the boat, and the moment of dawning that the boat was surrounded by police and at least one navy vessel. I didn't know whether to laugh or cry. Two men jumped overboard, one willingly, the other almost dragged in his wake. I knew they would soon be picked up or even drown; it was that kind of night.

The first explosion beneath my feet rocked the boat. Silence caught hold, and if the sea were a violent creature bent on domination then at that point its rage was muted, stunned into an aural halt. Another loud bang, and another, another...

I looked down beneath the grill and saw the reason: the fire. I had forgotten to put out the small fire I had built, and now it was out of control. Fireworks that had worked loose of the crates were being released from their earthly form, and like devils, they relished in the act of destruction. One loud bang almost tore the world apart, and whilst people were concentrating on the art of panic, I took it upon myself to do the only logical thing: I jumped into the sea.

I don't remember much after that. My mind was not with me as I gasped and spluttered between waves. I swam fifty, perhaps sixty yards before succumbing to the waves, and when I heard a the motor of a small boat coming towards me, I limply gave up. To be shredded in half by the police was perhaps the least of what I deserved.

The last thing I remember as the man who fished me out told me his first name, was the ship giving a sizeable groan. With the sense of gods and devils fighting over dominion of the water, suddenly exploding, fierce hot metal sent upwards, and it took all the might of the man who had rescued me to pull the small craft further out to sea as an empire fell.

23.

A Tale of a Knight on His Knees: The Final Confession

I AM NOT A bad man, nor am I evil. I have never danced with Professor James Moriarty. I have never even seen his soft shoe shuffle or his tango. I have neglected to be enamoured by the lure of overly sympathising with one of Colin Dexter's villains as they hold Morse's attention, although Barbara Flynn's portrayal as Monica Height was a good choice of casting as the first near femme fatale. Individuals are viewed as a series of heroic pauses, punctuated by one or two moments of madness in which people are hurt or their illusions shattered. When you die—when I die—will you remember the many good things I have done, teaching your children the fine art of literature in a world that harshly demands only for scientists, lawyers, politicians and shelf stackers? Will you only remember me for that one moment when I wouldn't take your side in an argument and gave you a look of brief contempt when you suggested that I should go fuck myself? Will you, my friend, remember the afternoons in The Pub and the help I gave you when you needed it most? Or will your memory of me be corrupted by the wife I stole from you?

This is my confession to you, my friend. I ran away from home because of one man's death, because of a past I could not escape, and because the most popular boy in my year tried to take credit for the poetry of a young girl he took to bed and then laughed in class as she took her life over the rejection. I could not stop her dying, but I fought as hard as I could to see her restored to her position as a great young poet. I took the Coventry allusion as friends turned against me for telling everyone who'd listen about the boy's behaviour.

My life is—perhaps was—a series of connecting lies, punctuated by the odd random moment of truth—the instance I grew a spine, a backbone, the devil of the conscience that would plague me.

Your father is a good man, my friend. I can hear the scoff catch in the back of your throat and you telling me that I know nothing. You had your issues with him, but remember—he stopped you from being dragged into a whole ship of mess which, in all honesty, was of your own making. I may have been the one to tell you to confess about the man you met in London, but it was your father who saved you. You were, and will always remain my friend, but your dad had your back when you should have served time.

Serving time—we all do that, don't we? We like to believe we are the masters of time, that our days and minutes are so regulated, so in tune with our lives, the seasons and the coming of the dawn that we are always surprised when the universe sends out a curve ball. We howl that it is unfair and that we have no time to be behind. Time is the master, the judge and the jury; it just depends on its mood and on how quickly it decides you should be punished. I must have been a particularly difficult man to reach a decision over; Time has judged me almost thirty years too late.

Your father pulled me from the water, did you know that? That night, off the coast of Gozo, as the ship's hold caught fire and the fireworks destroyed a huge consignment of heroin destined for the islands, your father pulled me out of the water and kept me safe as I related my story of the previous years and the insanity of the past few weeks to him. He listened as a father, not as a policeman. He listened with care, not judgement. He listened, and he dealt with the situation. He managed to keep me on the island, got me a job, changed my name, gave me a future…and I betrayed his trust, and he never knew.

My life was all right, but I had ambitions I could not deny. My schooling had stopped; I had wanted to go on and do A' Levels, go to university. I had wanted to see the world and get an education behind me. The former I had done, though I was unlikely to gain anything but a commendation in washing up and efficient food prep from a chef whose temper was as quick as his knife. I was free, I guess that was the main thing. I had survived. I could live without fear. But what is the point in freedom when it costs you the future?

Did you never wonder, my friend, how I paid for my education, how I got this house or the whisky I imported? Most of what I have came through the sales of books, through locking myself away for days on end in this very room and dissecting poetry lines and the people who created them. If you didn't at least have a suspicion of how I paid for it to begin with then I feel sorry for all those constables who have been at your side for years, for they have not had the right man leading them. I will be honest, my friend. I have not liked any of them. Perhaps my view is tainted by my own past, but they have all left me cold, no personality, not your type of person.

Take care of that new woman, though, the one from the Netherlands. She's got guts. She really knows how to get under a man's skin but make him feel used. Of all the women, she is the one for you—strictly professional. You could never truly make a woman happy, my friend, and I write that with the love of someone who calls you brother. You let your past dictate your future, and you try too hard to be a good man. I wonder if that is what made your son leave your side and not come back.

Who am I to judge a friend? I have screwed up more lives, including yours, than I could ever imagine. For what it's worth, I am sorry about your wife. I truly never meant it to happen. My crime was momentary; I needed money. I could be safe but I could never thrive. The answer lay in the potatoes I had placed in my bag before the boat went down. For several days, I had forgotten about them. I was exhausted after the weeks on the run. I had no reason to look at them, and if I had chucked them away after the first good meal I had eaten in weeks, as I sat with your mum and Dad in a café and stuffed myself to the point of being sick, then perhaps all the connections would have been severed, pulled apart the web.

But there was always the thin-faced man who saw me through the grills of the hold, who dragged me up the stairs. I know it was him who killed the woman who gave birth to me. I always knew it was him who had you in a dark corner, slowly sucking on your reason, your decency. I know it is him that has come for us both, my friend—you because you double-crossed him and sent him to jail, me because I am clumsy. I sank a ship carrying so much heroin it could have flooded the island. Who does he hate the most? Who has he focused his attention on whilst whittling away at time in a jail cell? I believe it is you.

That poor young girl, barely ready to grow breasts, certainly not prepared for the world and the lunatic takers who scream that everything should be theirs by right. What did she do to deserve the attention of a lying shit who took her virginity? I believe he did it with force, for she was not the kind of girl who gave it away, even under flattery; certainly not under teenage insistence.

If, in my life, I am redeemed by one action, I hope it is that as my prominence grew, I was able to put some of her work in an anthology of writing. Voices beyond the grave; voices that should have been more. There are hundreds, thousands of poems written every day but which never get seen, and they wither. They die a lonely, untouched death, unappreciated, never praised, never chewed over nor thought on, and why? Because the system is against it. It almost seems like a fluke of nature, the one poem that comes into a person's mind, a sense of uniqueness that if it had been in the hands of Keats, Auden or some other brilliant poet, would be lauded for all time. But that one single poem, written in the act of desperation, in pity perhaps, in self-loathing almost certainly...it just fades out of existence forever.

Do you remember the party we had when I published my first collection of poetry? What a night that was, both of us roaring drunk, there and then deciding to leave the girls as they started to feel the worse for the champagne we poured down their necks. We somehow managed to get a lift to Comino and carry on there—lots of late-evening beach partygoers all dancing on the small strip of triangular sand, and all because I'd written a book. I regret that.

I regret it because I should have saved the money and put it to better use—something I hope I atoned for with her poetry. In truth, she was better than me.

He didn't think so. He was jealous of her, that scumbag thief whose father was a big man, who coerced a headmaster to join in the charade, and who died for his sins. I took great enjoyment in taking that boy down. I had no quarrel with the girl, nice enough, a ghost-like presence in the classroom, never in trouble, meek, mild, painfully submissive, but put a pen in her hand and she was brilliant. It is just such a shame that her life, in many ways, was the start of the death of poetry. Could I call her passages in the book anything else?

The Death of Poetry. There it is in a nutshell. Boy takes credit for the work and insightful writing the girl has presented, the last vestige of the rape he committed as he used her like a cheap joke. That is what she was to him, a joke, a committed, senseless, brutal joke, and we were all the punchline. All those who fell in line with the bribe, with the threats, the possible beatings, the headmaster who saw the chance for prestige by having the school associated with the act of crime, and me, who sat in the classroom one day after everybody had left, with whispered names and veiled sarcasm poisoning my ear, and wondered what to do that was right, decent and honest. I had no choice. He had raped her and then raped her again. He was the cause of her death, but he was the golden boy of the local scene and his father had money.

Money my friend, is an evil, and I fell eventually for it as well. There is a fortune to be made in potatoes.

We have had our day, you and I. We are dinosaurs with a crippling debt to society. You owe it to yourself to seek redemption. I don't mean to meekly pass into the light. Remember the words, scream and shout, take the beast on with both hands if you must. Seize it by the throat, and should it look you in the eye, squeeze harder, for the cancer of society is not bad men who do terrible things; it is that we allow them to do so. We have had our day; we need to be absolved.

I had thought to leave this island; that was the plan. The day you told me about my mother, I was going to tell you that I was going to go back to England. I have my money, I have sold almost everything I own. I have lost my job over a girl. However, I don't think it is going to happen. Too much has transpired, too much death has occurred. She, our mutual friend in the bedroom, did not deserve to die that way. A whore—I use that word without pain or bitterness—should go willingly to the next encounter with a smile on her face and the wealth of an honest man in her purse. I saw the details on social media…you really need to do something about how such a crime is reported.

Where will you bury her? Or will you cremate her? Should this be read by you after my death and not as I hang myself out to dry in the public field, then please, do not bury me like a vegetable. Let my ashes be caught by a stiff sea breeze; let me go down in St. Julian's Bay if they will allow it.

A life it has been. From start to damn finish, it seems I shall be in the paper: a little baby with a needle sticking out of him, all there in black and white, a near junkie before I had learned how to gurgle, to now… How does this end? In noble self-sacrifice or screaming my innocence as they drag my life through the courts?

I sold the potatoes, my friend. I am guilty of that. I say 'the potatoes', but they had started to smell, go bad, by the time I remembered them. They should have gone straight in the bin. Nothing more would have been said. No one would have known, and all I would have been guilty of was being a terrible man, a letch, a despicable human being when it comes to relationships; hardly worth a sentence. No, I stupidly opened one up. I smashed it in anger against a wall. It was my way of letting go of all the frustration, of all that had gone between being born and being so far from home.

As the rotten, damaged chips fell to the floor, I saw a package, a clear polythene bag, inside. In it was powder. I am not a genius, but this I knew to be the reason for it all: the covert nature of the drugs bust at sea. Then the headlines hit home. Heroin!

What to do with several bags of illegal drugs… I should have given them to your father, earned praise perhaps, but I was greedy. I was never going to use it myself, but I saw the chance to make some money, and through a customer who came into the restaurant many times over the next month, I found a buyer. I am stupid, not a genius. I have no reason to believe otherwise.

I didn't recognise him, not until you finally saw sense and helped your dad with the raid up at the farm. It was the same man, thin-faced, the spider walking in human form, nasty venom, a bite that never lets go. You know when you have met the Spider; the bite stays with you forever.

He bought what I had. I paid for tuition and finally a university place. In effect, I had become a drug mule. I had crossed my own line. I had become a pawn of evil, selling my soul. I wish I had burned it all, but it gave me this life—just those few clear plastic packets stuffed with powder paid for all I see around me when I look up and into my study. The books, all thanks to powder. My degree, all thanks to powder. My Master's, my doctorate, my life, all thanks to someone willing to get high and eventually become a slave.

I hope my confession is not in vain. I am not a bad man, but I have done one very wicked thing, and now I am afraid. I know the thin-faced man is coming for me. I await death with open arms, my friend. I think it is time, for everything I have is worthless in hell.

Do not think badly of me. Look the Spider in the eye and break his neck if you can, for the Devil will surely welcome him, and you will find peace.

24.

A Tale of Two Men Who Went to War

THIS WAS MY job to finish, plain and simple. Too many webs had started to merge, to mingle and create a vast network of confusion, a labyrinth in which a spider can hunt down its prey, tire it out, exhaust it, make it start to panic, pant and eventually lie down and beg for the mercy of pincers that protrude from the spider's gaping jaw. Too many webs, one big network, strands being plucked at one end vibrating gently at the other. I could count on one person to finish this, and I wasn't even sure of myself.

I'd had no sleep all day. It would have been impossible with my nerves playing havoc. In all my years, I had never felt as on edge as I was at that moment.

The calm exterior may have fooled some; I hoped it deceived all. My boss…I was sure he was caught helpless somewhere on the outer fringes of the web, paid to look away, nothing more, nothing less. But how many others had, without their knowledge, been asked to do a favour for someone further involved?

I sat at the back of the café, the entrance just a few yards away, before me a small dry wall barricading me from the heat of the day and the sea which fell below my gaze and out over to the Three Cities. People came and went; the odd visitor who had ventured down this far into Valletta, serious about their trip being not just about sitting on arguably the finest beach in the whole of Europe but who also wanted to understand what Malta endured in the Second World War and through other dark times.

I drank more tea in those few hours than I ever wish to contemplate again. My mind raced with details, second- and third-hand memories, my companion in the craziness of the last few days, and the man who would kill me. Death was constant in all of this. My ex-wife, my friend, several policemen, a couple of boat owners, one silly girl who thought she had found a purpose…my sister slowly drowning as she got into difficulty, trying to impress, dying for her effort. All for what? For order? For a sense of having been alive?

***

I could take him now, as he sits there, cold and calculating but showing signs of nerves, the tapping of his fingers on the wall, picking at his shirt buttons. He is unravelling and he doesn't even realise it. I could pick up my rifle and I could take him. Oh, the screams, they would be loud. They would find him stone dead, his brain smeared against the café wall—a fitting end. He has been such a joy to slowly destroy, to shatter his opinions, his faith, all built upon his father's reputation, all for keeping him out of trouble. I wonder if he thinks I will leave the rest of his family alone once this day is done. I know he has sent his willing magpie to sit with them until he has me captured—does he really believe that she is enough, this young woman who owes me and yet does not even fully understand her own part in this?

Her family, I would wipe it out in an instant. I still may yet decide to do so. Payback is this game, all that time in jail, so many scores to settle, so many thieves of my time to add to the minutes I am awake and conscious of all they have done.

I am the Spider, and I am patient. Beware the anger of a patient man, they used to say. Death is even more patient. It lets you live, build up hope, friendships, a career. It senses just how much potential you have, and then, at the final moment, it extinguishes it before your eyes. All the seeds you have sown in fertile ground you see rise up. You watch it grow from strength to strength, but you never get to taste the crop. Like a match put out by a finger and a thumb, the light is soon gone, and all that remains is the smoking trail of what might have been.

Patience, my friend. You will soon reach the point where the vapour trail will turn to smoke, and you will see it turn ghostly, the faint whisper of life that once rested in your bones, your double-dealing, back-stabbing mind. I trusted you; you were to me a son. Now look, as you sit there in your linen jacket and matching coloured hat, looking for all purposes like the gentleman abroad. Gentleman, you are but a bullet away from being extinct.

***

I was never truly a patient man, nor was I a child. Yet in that café courtyard I sat. I looked at every person who came through the doors. I studied their mannerisms, I looked for any sign that they were there to watch me, see what move I made. Would I call for backup? Would I buckle under the pressure? Another hour to go; the evening was upon us, and inside the small café, I wondered if the lady who had poured me tea all afternoon had realised who I was. The charade of just waiting made me more nervous than I should have been.

Finally, I could stand no more. I got up from my seat, walked the few short steps to the back door of the café and paid in full my tab. If it was my last day on Earth then the tea had been a better companion than most. For the first time in my life, I tipped well—over and above. It wouldn't be any good to me now. I gave the young waitress my best smile, and she hesitantly gave me one back, but it was one covered in doubt. I had my suspicions that she might have thought I was some kind of pervert. Her eyes betrayed her; she could not look me straight in the face. *How many men have tried it on with you?* I wondered. *How many have promised you the world? How many have offered you everything? And how many have you wisely told to get lost? How many have you slapped, kicked, punched and spat at? Keep doing it—we as a gender are not worth your time.*

I thought about showing her my warrant card, but what would it have solved? She might think of me a little more kindly, but in the end, the only purpose it would serve was that when they found my body, she would have a better story to tell the local media and the world as it virtually witnessed my final downfall.

I said goodbye, raised my hat and walked off in the direction of the stairs that led to the tunnels once used as shelters from the Luftwaffe. I took one last look before I descended. The emancipated pony that was used to take tourists around the city caught my eye, and for the briefest of moments I felt a connection with the animal. It was here against its will, it was unhappy, ill-treated, and miserable. I felt a tug of remorse and allowed it to sweep over me. I turned my attention back to the stairs, the coolness of the caverns suddenly vibrant, unnatural and alarming.

I did not make a habit of coming here, not anymore, not since I was a child and my grandmother lost me. I had hidden in the shadows no more than a few feet from her, but she lost control over her emotions, and when I finally emerged, she beat me. Out of love, she said, but she beat me with all the power of a woman whose heart had been stretched too far.

***

That was not in the plan. You went before the allotted time. I was to get there first—why are you not sticking to the plan? My anger has been tested, time is sacrosanct, time is everything, down to the very last second. Without time being observed properly, events become blurred, mistakes get made, boats go down in the sea and children lose their limbs. Time is not to be messed with. Bad timing nearly cost that awful woman in the facility her life too soon. She had not suffered enough; she needed to be absolved of all her words, her blood-like memories.

Time is a god, and now I have to rush to meet you in the place as arranged. Leave it to the time that was agreed and you might walk back out into the sunshine. I so want you in the darkness. I want you to see me in the shadows. I want you to feel my teeth bearing down on you before I roll you in silk and hang you with all the rest of them.

Death is not meant to be rushed. It is not a firework sent hurriedly into the space above our heads, exploding so quickly that it barely has time to register in our minds what shape or colours it has formed. Death is the slow release of life, the heroin-filled veins working their way to the heart, squeezing it dry, creeping up on the mind, taking it to hell, slowly, surely, no second chances. Once you have the addict's taste, it stays in you. A couple of hundred years' worth of war for a simple flower, for land in the east, and it all boils down to the feeling of love that registers, the need that comes over in waves and the mask of living, slow-pulsed death that comes.

These people who rush everywhere, they make mistakes. The boy in the boat—what type of careless individual makes a small fire in a hold? What small-minded idiot forgets to put it out when he goes exploring? What fool puts traps out around his home and then wonders why his daughter loses a limb? What fool trusts a boy? The web is never good enough for them. They struggle, they fight back and waste energy. They spoil themselves, and the meal is never quite the same, the sense of victory somehow diminished.

This damn man. I will have you slowly staggering around in these tunnels until they find your lifeless body devoid of blood.

***

I had one shot. There would surely not be a second chance to hunt the Spider down before he scuttled away into the past again. He would only need one bullet to send me there so why should I allow him the same luxury of missing first time? I was under no illusion; I would die in here. The Spider might die also, but like the bee who managed to free himself and sting the assailant with eight legs, my act would be the death of me.

No signal this far down in the depths; no sign of anyone having been left behind from a party; no amorous teenagers or secretly lustful married couples having dared challenge the authority of the closing-time notice and to whom a night of exploration and several bottles of cheap wine were the least of the expectations on offer. In a way, that made me sad. I would not have wanted them to witness this, but it was always kind of fun to catch people where they should not be.

How was my constable holding up? I had sent her to keep an eye on my parents, but I knew damn well come the hour of this appointment, she would find a way to be here, to try to help. She was going to make a fantastic officer; my friend was right. All the others were just bad news, but she…she was something else. Was that the reason I left the café early, despite being warned to be in the tunnels at the set time? I could not bear to see her betray my trust?

Footsteps, almost silent and swift!

***

Footsteps, heavy but youthful!

I could see the detective no more than twenty yards in front of me. Revenge is such a petty thing. I was a businessman; I dealt with the supply and demand of a product. I saw to it that people had the product they needed or desired. Others help the economy by building cars that broke down, houses that weren't fit for human habitation, tower blocks that caught fire, trains that didn't go—they all get paid for their work. I do just the same. I sell dreams to the disillusioned and the weak. I am coming for you, dear detective.

***

I turned quickly on my heels, a noise in the distance catching my attention, but upon doing so, I saw just how close the Spider had come to me. For a man the wrong side of sixty, he had sure footing, and for the first time since his arrest, I looked directly into the Devil's face. I heard the noise again in the background. So did he. He swung around to see her not far behind us both. I would severely reprimand her for this, but also I could kiss her.

We both shouted, "Drop the gun," at the same time—the shout of a team working in tandem, and for a second, the Spider stopped moving. It was surreal; the web was fully charged. *Take me down, job done*, but he would go back to jail. She would see to that.

***

This surprises me. All that work and then to have the unexpected guest sail in and spoil the meal. I always knew she was good, this little magpie, but I thought the lawyer had told her what was expected of her. She was to behave, let this play out. She would survive; she would get the praise and the fortune; the riches were hers. I have one brief second to mull over all of this and choose my target. I take careful aim...and fire.

***

I watched as he took aim and fired. A near miss. She was all right, not even fazed. I didn't understand. Why didn't he take me? I was the one he had worked so hard to crack, to crumble into pieces. He had taken away all I cared for. Why not kill me? I figured later, in the cold light of day, that I just didn't want to know.

Our shots rang out in the echoing tunnels and met their respective targets easily. He stood firm in the face of death for a while, not moving, keeping almost too still. The only movement was the slow lowering of his arm, his gun falling to the floor as it gradually slipped from his fingers, the Spider losing its grip on life and embracing death with a certain faded dignity. He moaned one word in that time, as he looked at my colleague.

I had shot him in the spine. Apt, perhaps, the coward in me doing what he did best, releasing him from his life by metaphorically stabbing him in the back. I couldn't even look him in the eyes one last time. Aakster shot him in the head. She would have had her reasons, but as the dignity of the man faded, the blood oozed from his forehead. It dribbled down and dripped onto the floor—five, six, seven drops—before finally the empty vessel of the man followed suit and crumpled. The Spider was crushed.

I started to have serious words with Dutch but stopped as she took my hand and told me to formally reprimand her later. I asked her what his last word was; it seemed significant to her. It certainly wasn't aimed at me. She told me it meant magpie—her nickname when she was a child, handed down from her grandfather who was bestowed it in the heat of World War Two. He called her magpie.

As we approached the mouth of the tunnel, we both heard sirens. The day was over. Questions would be asked, but they could wait for now. I wanted to resign from the force—I was going to have to—but perhaps, like my friend, I could keep the reasons quiet for now, live a few more years.

Out of the corner of one eye, I saw the young waitress take some photographs on her phone. She looked awkwardly at me, and I wondered if she thought I should have been the one shot dead, the pervert who'd tried to chat her up as she cleaned and polished the counter and took my money. She asked Aakster if I was under arrest—had she caught a bad man? Dutch smiled at her and shook her head. "No," she replied. "He is just helping with our inquiries."

Epilogue

A Short Order of Thanks

It was a couple of weeks before we were able to scatter his ashes to the wind. The dry Maltese weather had been unfavourable to our cause. My boss kept his word; he had handed in his resignation the moment all the questions stopped, refused a commendation and was now working out his final few days before a well-earned holiday. He told me he might not come back.

I was asked to stay on, and I also refused. I wanted to go back home. I had a story to tell my family, a wrong to put right.

I never told my superior what had transpired when the lawyer spoke to me on the night of the double shooting. Both men were so cocksure I would comply with the request. *Stay away, keep your head down, and you will be a rich woman.* I'd never cared about money, but I agreed and went to my boss's side. I'd seen the policeman go into the room and shoot the boat owner and said nothing. Sometimes you have to allow a situation to play out. It was one less person who would get in the way.

The lawyer's body was found a couple of days after the death of the Spider—a suicide, apparently.

I watched the doctor's ashes catch the wind and sail over the end of St. Julian's Bay. Tomorrow, we'd do the same for the detective's ex-wife. I was going home at the end of the week, my time here on Malta an experience, a welcome conclusion to a story.

I took my boss's hand and prayed. The Spider was dead; several people had lost their lives through their connection to one man, but finally, after what had seemed a senseless search for justice, the man who was instrumental in the death of my aunt was dead. There would be no tears in hell tonight as Marshall Rhagodidae burned.

About the Author

Having been found on a 'Co-op' shelf in Stirchley, Birmingham by a Cornish woman and a man of dubious footballing taste, Ian grew up in neighbouring Selly Park and Bicester in Oxfordshire. After travelling far and wide, he now considers Liverpool to be his home.

Ian was educated at Moor Green School, Bicester Senior School, and the University of Liverpool, where he gained a 2:1 (BA Hons) in English Literature.

He now reviews and publishes daily on the music, theatre and culture within Merseyside.

Please visit www.liverpoolsoundandvision.co.uk

By the Author

Tales from the Adanac House

Black Book

The Death of Poetry

Beaten Track Publishing

For more titles from Beaten Track Publishing,
please visit our website:

http://www.beatentrackpublishing.com

Thanks for reading!